D0912614

Rotten Rapunzel

Rotten Rapunzel

Copyright © 2017 by Anita Valle

All rights reserved.

No part of this book may be used or reproduced in any manner whatsoever without written permission of the author except in the case of brief quotations embodied in critical articles and reviews. For information, e-mail the author at anitavalleart@yahoo.com

Cover art by Anita Valle

http://www.anitavalleart.com

ISBN-13: 978-1438264233
ISBN-10: 1438264232

Printed in the USA
First Edition, September 2017

Rotten Rapunzel

by Anita Valle

www.anitavalleart.com

Prologue

Snow White locked me up in this tower.

For fifteen years, I have been her prisoner. It's enough to drive a girl batty. When I was younger, she'd let me out sometimes to play in the snow. But not anymore. The kingdom is in peril, or so she says. We're in "dark days" now.

Ooh, I'm so scared.

What really burns me up is that this is *my* kingdom. Snowy could've been the queen but she chucked it years ago. So the title falls to me, her younger sister. It should be mine. It *will* be mine.

Someday, I'll escape my stupid tower. I'll cross The Wood that covers this kingdom and take back the palace. I'll become the queen I deserve to be and have a huge party with all of my friends.

And maybe even get a haircut.

Chapter 1

Snowy summons me to the window.

"Rapunzel!" she calls. "Let down your hair!"

You know, there's a door here. And stairs that wind up through the tower. She used to use them. But when a nasty queen took over our kingdom, Snowy sealed the door with ice. She's magic like that. My foot has not touched the snow for five years. And she doesn't even care.

I turn on the stool and slide away from the pipe organ. She's always interrupting my music, right at the good parts, too. I walk to the window, my long red hair dragging over the floor like a snake. I'm so deathly sick of doing this.

The window is of glass, two frigid panels that open like doors at the center. I push them out and lug my braid to the front of my shoulder. I gather up the long weave, looping it over my arm, and hang it from an iron hook that sticks out above the window. The braid rolls down to where Snowy is standing. I wait until I feel the tug, then I lurch back and pull, hand over hand, my braid hissing over the hook. It's like trying to haul up a cow - I guess. I've never actually seen a cow.

Snowy rises to the window and steps through. She's wearing a white fur coat all the way to her ankles, which makes her twice as heavy. And she always sticks her foot between the strands of my braid, which completely screws it up. I'll have to unravel the last two feet, brush it out, and braid it again.

"Did you get my gingerbread?" I ask, my breath whitened by the freezing-cold air that swoops in. I snap the window shut.

Snowy sets down her basket and slides out of her coat. She smells like fresh air and berries and faintly like pine. I've got a good nose.

"I tried," she says. "None of the bakers had any. Not much call for it right now."

I exhale loudly and walk back to my organ. It's a massive instrument, with rows of old pipes that cover the wall, rising tall at their center like fingers pointed in prayer. I lift my toes onto the pedalboard and press my fingers to the bone-white keys. Music fills the tower, high and whiny.

Snowy passes behind me and clomps down the stairs with her basket. The rooms here are round, each one stacked above the other. My organ room is highest, the only one that has a window. Our tower stands in the hills and Snowy says my music travels far across The

Wood. But no one comes near this tower, they're too afraid. Not of me, though. Of her.

The Snow Queen.

She comes back up the stairs now. I break off my music in mid-phrase and spin around on the stool. My braid curls around my feet like the tail of a cat.

"You could've *asked* the baker to make some gingerbread," I say. "I'm sure he would've done it for you."

"That would have taken hours," Snowy says. She's wearing a plain dress of white wool with long, tight sleeves. Her straight, black hair is loose and long, though not nearly as long as mine. Snowy is sixteen years older than me but we look almost the same age. Something about the ice magic that's in her, it's frozen even her youth.

I give her a withering look. "Well, it's not as if I'm going anywhere, is it? I could've waited for the gingerbread!"

"Then you would've been mad at me for taking so long."

"What did you get us for supper, some dumb bread and cheese?"

"Some figs too," she mumbles.

"I want gingerbread!" I slap my hand down on the keys, the organ growls. Snowy flinches back. "Rapunzel, please, it's such a long walk."

"Is that *my* fault?" I press a hand to my chest. "We could be living at the palace! And have all the food we

4

wanted. But no, you had to hole us up here like some kind of coward!"

"The kingdom is dangerous!" Snowy shouts. "Today I heard rumors-"

"I want GINGERBREAD!" I scream, grabbing the sheets of music off the organ and flinging them at her. They fan out and flap around before swooping to the floor. "Gingerbread, or no more tears."

Snowy looks at me. "You can't do that."

"Oh no? I don't *have* to cry." I fold my arms and smirk. I cry much less than I used to and I know it worries her. "How many tears have you got left?"

Snowy sighs. "One."

I cock my head. "Get my gingerbread. And then – maybe - I'll cry for you tonight."

Snowy rubs her face and looks tired. Slowly, she walks to the window. "Very well, Rapunzel. Let down your hair."

Chapter 2

Where has all the color gone?

The sun is sinking. It nearly touches the tip of the palace which sits down in the valley, past the long sweep of hills covered in sharp treetops. It's always so cold in here. But I stand at the window to fill my eyes with the pink and purple sky. Sunrise and sundown. The only times my world has color.

I remember when the world was green – it was so long ago. I would play in the clearing that surrounds this tower and my feet ran over something fluffy and warm that Snowy referred to as grass. It looked like green hair and smelled like sunshine. Then came the winter, with the clouds and the snow. And it never left.

The winter grew to cover the kingdom. In The Wood, even the pines are gray now. Black, white, and gray – that's all I see outside my window. The sky is often curdled with clouds, ready to release more sickening snow. I hate white. I hate it so much.

Chilled, I turn away from the window. Snowy hasn't gotten back with my gingerbread. The days just feel eternal sometimes. I pick up a candle on its little tin plate and carry it down the rickety stairs. The room just below is our bedroom, cold and dark as a cave. There's a wide bed for me and Snowy – I sleep on the right. We've also got a trunk for our clothes, a table with two candles, and a box where I keep my books.

I set the candle on the table and kneel in front of the box of books. It's actually a crate. Snowy's told me, a few thousand times, that I slept in this crate as a baby. I don't know why she thinks I'd care about that. I don't even care about my twin sister who was stolen from us when we were infants. It's just a story I've heard too many times. Snowy's full of them.

But I like my books. I grab the one on top and crawl onto the bed. My braid lies on the floor and goes up the steps, the end of it still upstairs. I just started a book about a poor peasant girl who lives on a farm but wishes for a grand adventure. Lucky girl, it'll probably happen to her. Sometimes, I think Snowy really regrets that she taught me to read. If it wasn't for books, I'd have no idea how abnormal my life is.

For example, from books I have learned that most children grow up with a mother and a father. And if two girls are born from the same mother, they're called sisters. But even though Snowy says she and I are sisters, we don't come from the same mother. I try but

I still can't understand it. Snowy's mother was once queen of this kingdom. So was *my* mother, but she was a different lady, named Cinderella. Cinderella was Snowy's stepmother. That confuses me even more.

I wish I had a mother and father. They sound like nice things to have.

From books, I have also learned about men and boys. And sometimes – it's pretty rare – I'll even see a man down in The Wood when I'm looking out my window. Small and far away, but my eyes are good. They're so funny! They don't grow their hair long. They have strange, low voices and thick arms. They wear a tight sleeve on each leg (called pants, I believe.) And hair grows right on their faces! I'm dying to see a man up close but I know if I do, I'll either burst out laughing or run away screaming. Neither of which would be very polite.

My father was a man. His name was Edgar and he was the king. I never saw him, he's long dead, just like my mother, Cinderella. Snowy says I shouldn't miss them, they were both bad people. But I don't believe her. I really wish I could've seen them, at least once. Just to know what they looked like....

No. I blink rapidly. I'm not going to cry. But gob dash it, a tear drops onto my cheek. I hop off the bed, run down to the kitchen, and let the tear fall into a cup. I promised Snowy, after all. She'll freeze it and sell it later. That's how she gets our food and clothing and other supplies.

Because, apparently, most girls don't cry magic tears.

Chapter 3

Snowy is helping me wash my hair.

It's a huge job. We do it in the kitchen. It's the smack-bottom room of this tower and has a small iron stove. Snowy puts two kettles on top of the stove and fills them with ice. I wish she could shoot hot water from her hands, but nope, just ice and snow. She builds a fire to melt the ice inside the kettles. That's how we get all our water.

"How's the gingerbread?" She's crouched at the washtub about six feet away, rinsing my hair. We have to wash it in sections, my forty feet of hair doesn't fit in the tub all at once. So we start with my head and work back, dunking, scrubbing with scented soap, rinsing, then moving on to the next section.

"Pretty good," I say. "But now my head's getting cold." The kitchen is the only room that ever gets warm, but it's not warm enough. It's so depressing down here, there are no windows, just a bunch of drippy candles that make everything look wobbly and orange.

"So throw a towel over your head," Snowy grumbles. She's got sparkles of sweat on her forehead as she lifts the sodden bundle of hair out of the tub and squeezes the water from it. Towels are spread across the floor to hold the clean hair while she washes the rest. She drops the wet section, limp as a dead animal, and lifts the next eight feet or so of my hair.

"You need to change the water." I pinch off a morsel of soft, sticky gingerbread and slip it into my mouth. The water must be changed twice with each washing.

Snowy sighs. "No, I don't."

"I can smell the dirt."

"No, you can't!"

I turn on the stool, look at the water, then her. I raise my eyebrows. "You are *not* putting my hair in dirty water."

Snowy sighs again, longer this time. "You're such a brat!" She picks up the washtub with an angry grunt. She's got to go all the way to the top floor and dump it out the window. Oh well, not my fault. She could've gone right outside if she hadn't iced up the stupid door.

I hum and chew on my gingerbread while she clunks up the stairs, resting the tub on each step. I wish I could play my organ but I have to stay in the kitchen all day and let the warm air dry my hair. I can't even walk when it's wet, it's too heavy. Tonight, Snowy will comb it out and braid it again. I'm glad we do this only once a week, I get so tired of sitting on this stool.

About ten minutes later, she stomps back down with the empty tub. "You should wash your own hair!" she fires at me.

My fingers are sticky and I lick the sweetness off them. They smell like ginger and sugar.

"Don't lick your fingers!" Snowy snaps.

I keep licking. She drags the second kettle of water off the stove. "You could've gotten this down for me, you know, or put in some more firewood!"

I mimic her voice in high-pitched tones. " 'You never help out around here!' "

"Well, you don't!" Snowy shouts. She heaves up the kettle and tips it into the tub. "I do everything while you just sit there! You could learn to cook and clean a little!"

"But I'm a princess!" I give her a prim little smile.

"Spoiled rotten is what you are," Snowy says as she gathers up more of my hair. "Hunter wouldn't have stood for it."

Oh no, *please*, not the Hunter stories! I'm so deathly sick of them. Her handsome, honey-sweet lover who died when a magic mirror exploded. Boohoo, it's been fifteen years, get over it.

"Are you done yet?" I say to distract her.

"I've still got another six feet to do," she growls, lathering in the soap. "I hate your hair." She has said that for years. "One of these days I'm going to cut it off while you're sleeping!" She has said that for years too.

I'm not worried. I never let her touch my hair as a child. I liked having it long. And something about the sound of the scissors would freak me out. I threw crazy tantrums, loud and violent, to keep her from cutting my hair. It worked every time.

And if she couldn't control me then, she certainly can't do it now.

Chapter 4

I'm playing my organ while Snowy paces behind me. "I need you to cry, Rapunzel!"

"Not now!" I yell above the music. Nothing happens until I finish my sonata.

"It's past noon already. If you don't cry, then we don't eat today! All I need is one – oof!" Snowy trips on my braid, lying in bundles around the room, and kicks it aside. "Stupid hair!"

"Get off it!" I shout. My fingers pump the keys, the music throbs against the wall, warbling high and grumbling low at once. I practice six hours a day. I mean, what else have I got to do?

I'm wearing a thin, silky dress of pale peach. It used to be Snowy's until I decided it looked better on me. I feel like a princess in it. It's not heavy enough for our endless winter, but my playing keeps me warm. The organ is a four-limb exercise.

Snowy prowls around in her white fur coat. With a huffy sigh, she stops at the window and stares out for a minute.

"Rapunzel! Look!"

I glance over my shoulder. "What?"

"I see one!"

I hop off the stool, hop over my hair, and run to the window. "Where? Where?"

"Down in The Wood. Look. Under the yew trees, that space between them. Do you see her?"

I do. A fairy, far below us in The Wood. She's got her back to us, so we can only see her wavy brown hair and delicate wings. Her feet hover a few inches above the ground and she gives off a gentle glow.

I'm breathless watching her. She's so beautiful. I wish she'd turn her head so I could see her face. I wish she'd come up here and talk to me. We could be friends. I've never had a friend.

Snowy's eyebrows draw lower. "She's so stiff."

"Stiff?"

"I mean she's not moving. She's facing one direction, not looking right or left. And her posture is rigid. I think she's watching for something."

"For what?"

The fairy turns her head, snaps her wings, and shoots into The Wood. The trees prevent me from seeing where she goes.

"They're everywhere now," Snowy says, turning back into the room. "It's so strange."

"What is?"

"The fairies. They're appearing in the kingdom, especially in the towns. It's no longer uncommon to see one."

"Why? Why are they here?" I follow her across the room to the stairs, stooping for a moment to pick up my braid. I loop it over my elbow and let the end dribble down the steps behind me.

"Dark days have fallen," Snowy says.

"Oh, will you stop saying that!" I cry. "What's *happening* out there, just tell me!"

Snowy remains quiet as she glides down the stairs, fingertips hovering just above the railing. Like always, our bedroom is chilly and dark, only one candle burning on the small table. Snowy looks at me. "Get your cloak and come sit on the bed."

I grab my cloak of brown bear fur off the chair where I left it and wrap it over my shoulders. It's soft and heavy and solidly warm. I crawl onto the bed and fuss with the cloak until it covers most of me. But Snowy doesn't join me at the headboard. She perches on the side of the bed, folds her hands, and faces the wall as she speaks.

"When I brought you to this tower, I left the palace empty, without a king or queen to rule the land. I couldn't go back. Dangerous men were hunting for me and my ice magic was not yet strong."

She has told me about these dangerous men before. A brutal gang of criminals who call themselves The Dwarves. She was their friend at one time. Until they turned against her.

"But your power is strong *now*," I say. "So why can't we go back?"

Snowy lifts a hand to silence me. "I watched from this tower as war broke out across the kingdom. I didn't care at all. I was grieving for my Hunter. I never even got to bury his body." She looks at me, her eyes glossed with a layer of tears.

I exhale. "Yes, I know about Hunter. What happened next?"

Snowy turns away. "Nothing. Why should I tell you? You don't care about anything."

"You want my tears or not?" I say.

She makes a disgusted sound but continues. "The war lasted for months. I saw fires and heard screaming, mostly around the palace. The Wood burned from one side to the other. I stood at the window, with you in my arms, and watched the kingdom turn black."

"We didn't get attacked here?" I ask.

"The palace was the target. Not a small tower lost in the hills. Occasionally, a foolish band of men would find their way to this clearing." Her pale cheeks round as she smiles. "I practiced my magic on them. I learned how to aim and manipulate the ice. I wrapped it around their faces until they suffocated. I impaled them on spikes

17

that shot up from the ground. I trapped them in blocks of ice but left their heads free and I made them tell me what was happening in the kingdom before they froze to death."

I'm sitting quite still now. Well, that was... super creepy. I didn't know she could do that – kill people with her magic. She only uses it to fill the kettle, block the door, seal the cave that leads to our clearing. Snowy is a boring person who uses her magic for boring things. I've never seen her do anything like that.

"How'd the war stop?" I ask, more respectfully.

Snowy shrugs. "I was never quite sure. It got quiet again. I started to venture out for food, once I felt sure of my magic. Little by little, I heard about the new queen."

"Who is she?" I ask.

Snowy sighs. "I haven't met her. Don't plan to, either. She is cruel and vicious, nobody likes her. I'm surprised she's lasted this long."

"So, it's just her, no king?"

"No, there's a king too. But nobody talks about him, it's the queen who holds the land."

"Then let's take her down!" I say, thumping the bed with my hand. "We'll go there and you can bury her in a block of ice. And we'll take back the palace!"

"Why?"

"Why not?"

"I don't want to go back there. And see the room where Hunter...." She closes her eyes.

I roll my own. "And that's why we've stayed here all this time? This doesn't explain your 'dark days,' you know."

Snowy turns blazing eyes on me. "The queen doesn't like young girls, especially ones about your age. They're being found dead all over the kingdom. Is that dark enough for you? Horrible deaths too, slashed and mangled and left to bleed in the snow. So, excuse me for precaution but I *don't* want that happening to you!"

I'm silent. My eyes dart around while I think. Those girls - young girls like me. I've never even seen a young girl. But in some of my books there are drawings. In one book, there's a lovely picture of a girl with pink cheeks and long yellow curls. I used to stroke her image with my fingers and imagine we were friends. We did everything together, she was very real to me. So, it is her that I imagine now, dead in the snow, her yellow curls spread around her.

"How... how is this happening?" I ask.

Snowy rubs her eyes. "The queen has magic, I think. One of the reasons I'm not sure I can face her. She can control things. There is talk of a very large animal who does her bidding. That's what's hunting the girls."

"What do you mean, a large animal? What kind of animal?" My eyes are wide.

"I haven't seen it myself. But everyone calls it the Beast."

Chapter 5

Well. That was something. Actually, I feel pretty sick about it. But I don't tell Snowy.

Snowy's out getting food. I gave her a teardrop, not too hard after that story. Now I'm sitting on the floor of my organ room with my back to the stone wall. Sometimes I just run out of things to do. I jiggle my ankles and try to imagine what the Beast looks like. And what I'll do if it ever comes here.

"Rapunzel! Let down your hair!"

I freeze, every bone, every muscle, as if Snowy just zapped me with her ice.

Because that *wasn't* Snowy's voice.

I stand slowly, sliding up against the wall. My heart bumps and crashes around. I don't know what to do. I need Snowy! Unless... unless I heard it wrong and that *was* Snowy. But it didn't sound like-

"Rapunzel! Let down your hair!"

No, that's not Snowy. I crouch and hug the wall. I'm scared. I'm shaking. I think about running to my bedroom and hiding inside a trunk. But my hair won't fit.

"Come on, Rapunzel, I know you're up there."

The voice sounds... different. Not scary, exactly. But deep and strange. I start to wonder what's out there, what it looks like. But the fact that it's calling to me – by name – is more than I can handle. I stay crouched and hope it goes away.

"Just come to the window, Rapunzel. I won't hurt you."

My fear shrinks a tiny bit. It said it won't hurt me. Then it can't be a bad thing that's out there. Maybe I can look for a second.

I stand up and inch along the wall toward the window. I won't step in front of the glass. I just sort of lean sideways to get one eye past the wall. And I see it. Down in the snow, a figure, dark hair, an upturned face – and I immediately drop to the floor again.

"Ha! Saw you!" the voice cries, jubilant. "You've got red hair, very long. I've seen your mama use it to get up there. And I've heard your music. I just want to talk to you. Don't worry, I'm a nice guy."

I'm still scared but curiosity is taking over. I want to have another look. Slowly, I rise in front of the glass, my heart ready to stomp right out of me. I look at the figure.

It's a... man, I think. He's wearing pants and boots. But he doesn't have a beard. His eyebrows are quite noticeable, thick and dark, like his hair. He raises a hand to greet me and smiles, which startles me. His smile is nothing like Snowy's. It looks happy and shows a lot of teeth.

I don't smile back but I'm fascinated. I've never seen another person this close. I want him to leave. But I also want to keep looking at him.

"Hello there!" he calls. "Why not open the window so I don't have to shout?" His tone is cheerful. And a word suddenly enters my head: *friend.* I have always wanted a friend, a real one I can see and touch. Friends are good things to have, they make you laugh. And I never laugh at all.

I push one side of the window open, just a few inches. "Are you a friend?"

"I beg your pardon?" He takes two steps closer to the tower and lifts a hand to his ear.

I push the window out more. "Are you a friend?"

"Well... I'm friendly!" He grins. "My name's Kay. I've been watching you from The Wood. It was your music that got my attention. You play amazingly."

I can't stop looking at him. "Are you a man?"

"I am now! Sixteen on my last birthday. How about you?"

"Fifteen." My voice doesn't sound like me, soft and unsure. "But I'll be sixteen pretty soon."

"Have you ever been out of that tower?" he asks with a serious face.

I shake my head. I don't bother telling him that I used to play in the clearing. It doesn't count for much.

His face changes in a way I don't understand. A bit sad? A bit worried? But why should he be worried for me?

He smiles again and it's a nice one. "So, no one has ever seen your pretty face but me?"

"Am I pretty?" From books, I have learned that being pretty is very important. The pretty girls always have lots of friends and even if bad things happen to them, they still find happiness in the end.

"Quite pretty. If you leaned out a little I could see you better. Unless you're still scared of me."

I'm really not, anymore. I push the window as far as it goes and lean out on my arms. Unexpectedly, I feel the urge to smile. So I do.

He smiles back. "Now let's see the hair."

He wants to climb up. But I'm not completely stupid. Miss-Snowy-Snow-Queen will freak out if she comes home and finds a stranger here. I don't know this guy very well, but enough that I don't care to see him impaled by an icicle.

I shake my head.

"You don't trust me. I get it," Kay says. "Tell you what! I'll come back tomorrow. And I'll bring you a little present. What would you like?"

"I like gingerbread," I say. "But you shouldn't come back here. Make sure you smear away your footprints when you leave. If Snowy finds out, she'll be really mad."

"Is that your mama?"

"No, my sister, Snow White."

Kay stares at me. "What did you say?"

"What?"

"Did you call her Snow White?"

"Yes."

"The one who used to be the princess?"

"Yes."

Kay looks stunned. "So, it *is* her. She's the Ice Witch."

I frown. "The Snow Queen."

"Same thing. I knew she lived somewhere up in the hills, but I didn't know who she was. I've been watching her from the trees for weeks. But you were a surprise. It looked to me like she was keeping you as a prisoner."

"Well, that's true enough."

"I wanted to talk to you alone, to see how things were. I thought I might be able to help you. But first! You need to trust me. So, I'll come back tomorrow and bring your gingerbread. And we'll talk some more. Just do me a favor, would you? Please don't tell your sister I was here."

I wouldn't dream of it.

Chapter 6

I wake up. I can't see a thing, just unbroken black. I hate sleeping without a candle, it's like being blind. But when you have as much hair as I do, you can't risk a fire.

I heard something. Something upsetting. It sounded like... oh, I don't know. My sleep-soggy head is already forgetting, washing it away like a dream. But I know in my bones it wasn't.

I sit up and listen. There it is - a scream. Starts low, then peals out long and high. In music, we'd call it a crescendo. My scalp crinkles from one side to the other and I'm bit hard by fear. I drop into the mattress and shove my body against Snowy's.

"Wake up, wake up, wake up!"

"What's the matter?" she asks sharply.

"I hear something!"

The bed squeaks as Snowy shifts herself up. When I try to speak, she hushes me. We wait without a twitch in the black silence.

Another scream, thin and distant, ripe with frantic fear. I feel sickened.

"Stay there," Snowy says. I feel the weight of her blankets flung over me as she leaves the bed.

"Where are you going?" I whimper.

"Just stay there!" She gropes her way around the bed and climbs the stairs to the organ room. I burrow under the blankets and curl into a ball. How could she just leave me here?

Barely a minute passes before I hear her again.

"Rapunzel?" she calls from the top of the stairs.

"What?"

"I need you to let down your hair."

My eyes open wide. "You're going OUT there?"

"Hurry, Rapunzel!"

My legs get tangled in the covers and I fall hard out of bed. "Ugh - coming!" I scrabble on all fours to gather up my braid, bunching it against my stomach. It's cold from the floor. Hunched over my loops of hair, I patter up the stairs in my bare feet.

My organ room is freezing cold! She's got the window wide open and the frozen air dumps in and spreads. She's standing at the window in her white fur coat, the wind lifting long strands of her hair.

"It's a young girl," she says without looking back.

I stagger forward. "You can see her?"

"I can tell by the screams. The sound is moving. I think something is chasing her in The Wood."

27

I gasp. "Do you think-"

"I don't know!" Snowy says. "Now get over here and help me!"

I hurry to the window and toss my braid out over the hook. Snowy climbs onto the sill and takes careful hold of the dangling end. Letting her down is always harder than bringing her up. I lean back and release the braid, a handful at a time, my bare feet planted to the frozen floorboards. My toes go numb in seconds.

When the tension on my braid slackens, I yank it back and throw it into the room behind me. Then I rush to the window.

Snowy stands below me in the clearing. She walks forward, her boots leaving shallow prints in the snow, the fine hairs of her fur coat floating and quivering. She nears the edge where the ground becomes scruffy with weeds and small trees before it drops down the side of the hill.

Another scream lifts out of The Wood and Snowy turns her head to the sound. She lifts both arms and spreads her fingers in the moonlight. And then things start to get interesting.

Snow begins to rise from the ground. It floats up toward her hands in tiny white bits. Then the snow just behind her drifts upward. All around her, all around the clearing, snowflakes are rising into the night. They lift higher and higher until they're flitting past my window.

It looks just like it's snowing, except that it comes from the ground instead of the sky. An upside-down snowfall.

Snowy spreads her arms. The snowflakes rise faster, thicker, and start to swirl. Her power has reached The Wood where the snow is now floating out of the treetops. Bare patches of earth appear like bruises on the ground as she lifts the snow into the air.

The snow spirals around her, thickens and spreads, a cyclone that constantly grows. I can barely see Snowy, now, behind the whirling white. I step back because the snow is beating the right side of my window frame and shooting into the room. I grab the glass doors and tug them shut. What is she doing? It looks like a blizzard out there.

A blizzard....

I look at the snow stuck against the wall near my organ, dusting the pipes in sparkles. And at the window again. A blizzard. So dense and furious it can't be seen through. You can't walk in this kind of blizzard. You can't even see what's in front of you.

She's blinding it. If something – the Beast or whatever – is chasing a young girl, it can't see where it's going, now. Neither can the young girl, of course, but it will give her a chance to hide or at least distance herself from her pursuer.

Snowy is trying to save her.

I hug my nightdress to my body, amazed. I had no idea Snowy could do something this big. She told me she was the reason our kingdom is always cold, but I never saw her pull a blizzard out of her sleeve, so to speak. Is the whole kingdom going through this? Can she really do that? For the first time ever, I feel a teensy bit afraid of Snowy.

And I'm shivering. I run on tiptoes down to our bedroom and dive under the blankets, huddling in a spot still partially warm from our bodies. I listen to Snowy's blizzard swoop and wail around the tower. It's almost as scary as the screaming was.

Oh yes. She is the Snow Queen.

I have to get out of here.

Chapter 7

"Oh my stars, I'm exhausted." Snowy slumps in a kitchen chair, her feet held up by the washtub, turned over. I'm standing by the stove, waiting for water to boil. She asked me to fix her a strong cup of tea. Under the circumstances, I decided not to give her an attitude about it.

"How do you do that?" I ask carefully. "How do you not freeze to death?"

Snowy smiles at me. She came in pale, with blue lips and fingers, but her eyes blazed triumphant. I think she's proud of herself.

"It wasn't easy," she says. "I sustained it for an hour. Thought my arms were going to break off!"

"Do you have to lift your arms?" I ask.

"It helps. To direct the flow of magic. It's always come from my hands." She grimaces and massages her fingers.

"But how do you not freeze to death?"

"It's heavy work, lifting that much snow. Like pushing rocks uphill for an hour. It keeps me warm. But I did start to shiver at the end. I was weakening."

"Do you think it worked?" A sputtering trail of steam flows out of the kettle and I grab a dishcloth and lift it off the stove. I have Snowy's cup ready on the kitchen table. I tip the kettle and pour, using a small wire strainer to catch the tea leaves. It smells hot and bitter, but that's how she likes it.

Snowy sighs. "I don't know. I'll go out when the sun comes up and look around. Ask if anyone was in trouble last night. I hope the fairies were helping her too."

"Why?" I set the cup on a saucer and carry it to her. "You don't do stuff like that. You always say you don't care about the kingdom."

"I don't," Snowy says. "But it sounded like a girl your own age to me. For all I know, it could've been your sister. Our sister."

"Oh...." I didn't think about that. I tend to forget about my twin sister. After all, I have no memories of her. But when I do think of her, I feel resentful. Wherever she is, I'm sure her life is better than mine. I bet she lives in a village and has lots of friends. I bet she wasn't locked away and raised as a prisoner. I bet she has seen things like horses and carriages and streets and shops. I bet she goes outside whenever she wants.

"Did she look like me?" I ask.

Snowy shrugs. "She was just a baby when I lost her. I ran out of the palace with both of you in my arms. Your little heads were right under my chin, you with red hair, she with brown. And then that horrible creature stole her from me - Cinderella's fairy godmother."

This part I've heard before. And that Snowy never saw them again. We don't know where my sister is or what name was given to her. But the fairy – Godnutter, she's called – is considered a disgrace by her kind. Fairies are supposed to do good things for people, not go around snatching their babies.

Snowy sips her tea and sighs at its warmth. I'm sitting on the kitchen table, my braid hooked over my swinging foot. I think about the blizzard again.

"Can you make it snow from the sky?" I ask.

Snowy shakes her head. "I can't form clouds in the sky. That's bigger than me. All I can do is freeze the moisture in the air and tell it where to go. The kingdom remains in winter because I keep the air as cold as possible. I barely have to think about it. This land is mine, whatever that lunatic at the palace may think. Hunter's death froze my heart and the kingdom froze with it. It knows I am its queen."

"Then we should be at the palace!" I cry. "Where the people could see your power and respect you! And I could be a princess and have friends!"

"I'm not going back there," Snowy says firmly. Her brow creases. "My power doesn't seem to affect the palace, at least not in the gardens. The roses bloom every year when it should be summer. I can't freeze them."

"Why not?"

Snowy shrugs. "An enchantment? I don't know. This kingdom has many secrets. Magic has a way of... hibernating, I guess. And then emerging when it's needed. When I was a girl, I scarcely saw magic at all. Now it's everywhere, like the fairies."

"I know, dark days." I roll my eyes.

Snowy ignores me and sips her tea. Her smile returns. "I wish Hunter could've seen me last night. I saved someone – at least, I think I did. He would've been pleased. And even more so-" her eyes narrow "-I wish Cinderella could've seen me. She thought me useless. But look at me now." She swirls her finger into the steam rising from her cup and it freezes into a little spiral around her finger. She smiles at it for a moment and then closes her hand, shattering it.

"Did you ever see her do anything good? Even a little bit?" I don't like it when Snowy talks dirt about my mother. I know she wasn't perfect, but nobody's evil all the time, right?

"Hmm...." Snowy takes a thoughtful sip of her tea. "Let me see... uh no! You're mother never did anything good."

I thump down from the table. "You're lying!"

"She's dead, Rapunzel. Let it go."

"She wasn't evil!"

"She was a selfish, crazy, murderous woman who ruined my life and my family. When she died, nobody cared! Nobody mourned! Because *nobody* ever loved Cinderella." Snowy's cheeks, pale before, are now lit with a hot reddish glow.

My eyes flood with tears. "I hate you!"

Snowy sits up and points at me. "Blink!"

I try not to but the blink still comes. Two heavy tears slip onto my cheeks. They freeze instantly and fly across the room into Snowy's outstretched hand.

"I'll sell these when I go out today." She smiles at me.

Chapter 8

I let her out the window at daylight. Finally! I haven't forgotten that Kay promised to come back. And bring me gingerbread. I needed Snowy gone, as soon as possible.

I put on my favorite warm blue dress while I wait. Snowy bought it for me a year ago and I love it. It's made of fine wool, the color of blueberries, and hugs my body with softness. I spread the skirt and sit at the organ, then change my mind about playing. I'm afraid I won't hear Kay when he comes. Pity though, the gusts swooping around the tower must be filling the windchest nicely. The air flows through valves in the outer wall and gets stored in a chamber beneath the pipes. On a windy day, I can play quite loudly.

I fetch my book and try to read about the farm girl. But it's hard to concentrate. My life is about waiting, always waiting. Each day, I wait for Snowy to come home. I like it when she leaves but I also like it when she comes back. When she takes too long, I start wondering what would happen if she never returned. What would I do? It scares me to think about it.

The morning slides along, a slow march. I sit cross-legged on the floor with sheets of music in my lap, humming the melodies while my fingers play notes in the air. I'm itching to play the organ, to fill the lonely silence. I hate silence almost as much as I hate white.

"Rapunzel!"

It's him. I run to the window and shove it open. He's down there like yesterday, except now he's standing on dirt littered with branches. I guess Snowy didn't put the snow back after her blizzard.

I smile. "Hello."

"Hello to you too!" He grins at me. He's bundled up against the cold, a black cloak wrapped up to his chin and a hat of grey fur pulled down to his eyebrows. I like his smile, big and white. It makes me feel happy inside.

He holds up a wrapped package in his mitten. "Got the gingerbread."

"Oh! Can you toss it?" I hold out my hands.

"That's no way to treat a lady. I'd much rather come up to you. If you'll let down your hair for me...." He lifts his eyebrows and waits.

I hesitate.

"I won't hurt you, Rapunzel. I swear on this loaf of scrumptious bread that I won't hurt you." He holds up a hand while he says this and the underside of his cloak is grey fur like his hat. I think it might be ermine.

"I know. I'm just worried about Snowy catching you here. She might do something horrible. She made that blizzard happen last night, you know."

"I know. The whole kingdom knows. Why did she do it?"

"Well...."

"Wait, don't tell me! Let me come up first."

"But what if she comes back? There's no way out of here except by this window. The door's frozen over."

I point to the base of the tower where the ice grows up in sharp white fingers, covering the door. The whole bottom half of the tower is crusted over like that.

Kay nods at it, frowning. "Not very welcoming, that's certain. And those huge icicles hanging from the roof, they could kill somebody." He rubs his chin with his thumb. "Well then! I guess you'll have to come down to me.

I gasp.

"Can you use your hair to get down?" he asks.

"I don't know! I never tried. There's no one up here to counterbalance me."

"Hmm...." Kay stares at the hook above my window. "It would be risky. I don't want you to hurt yourself. Tell you what! When I come back tomorrow, I'll bring a rope. And we'll go somewhere! What would you like to do?"

My fingers tingle. I can't believe it. "I – I want to have an adventure. And see things."

"Like what?" he asks, grinning.

"Like a town. A real town with houses… and people walking around. I want to see people!"

"Sure thing! We'll go to the nearest town. Your, uh, your hair might raise a few eyebrows, though."

"Why?"

"Most girls don't grow it quite that long."

I laugh. "Oh, I'll manage it! Do you live in this town where you're taking me? Will you show me your house?"

Kay's expression changes. "Um… I might." He's not smiling now. "I mean, I could show you where I live. But it's a pretty long walk. I don't live in a town."

"Well, where do you live?"

Kay's eyes drop away from me and he shrugs. "I live at the palace. I'm sort of the prince."

Chapter 9

Snowy brings supplies back with her. Small sacks of flour and barley, chestnuts and dried apple slices, a ball of yarn in bright blue, scented soap for my hair, and more candlesticks. I have to haul up the basket first and then her.

"My tears sold for a high price today," I remark as she steps through the window. Snowy doesn't reply, her face looks like a brick.

"Was someone here? Was a man here?" she fires at me. My stomach gives a sickening sudden drop.

"There are boot prints in the dirt. They weren't there when I left." She stands with her back to the window, her mouth a tight line.

Think fast. Something she'd believe. "Oh, it was that man. The one who helped you after we came here. And built my organ."

Snowy frowns. "Wurley? He hasn't been here since you were a baby. What did he want?"

"To see if we needed anything." My heart's pounding so hard I can hear it. I know it's not a strong story. When Snowy first came to this tower we had nothing, not even chairs. Then she happened on a man in The Wood who had once been a palace servant. He was willing to help her and brought us things, little by little. The organ was his idea, something he found in an abandoned church and brought as a gift for Snowy (I think maybe he had a thing for her). But she seldom played, not wanting to draw attention from outsiders. By the time I learned, her ice magic was stronger and she no longer feared the world. I don't remember the man, I was too little. He's just another one of Snowy's stories.

"What did he look like?" Snowy asks.

Oh sugar. "Um... old." I figure that must be true by now. "Sorry if I don't have a better description. I don't exactly get to *see* many people, do I?"

"Did you speak to him?" she asks.

I shake my head. "I was too scared. I ran to my room and hid until he left."

Snowy looks satisfied. She pulls the window shut and slides out of her heavy coat. "He was a good servant. It must've been quite an effort for him to climb up here. Maybe he wanted to warn us about the Beast. I'll stop by and see him next time I go out." She picks up the basket and walks to the stairs. "Is it too much to ask you to help me put the stuff away?"

41

I fold my arms. "That's it?"

"What?" She's already heading down.

"You'll stop by and see him when you go out. That's not fair, Snowy. That's really not."

"Oh my stars, what now?" Snowy says, coming back up a step.

"It's not fair. If you get to go out and see people, then I should too." This whole thing with Kay has me thinking. I should just be allowed to go out and see him without all of this sneaking around. We're going to see a village tomorrow and maybe even the palace! I had no idea know we had a prince my own age. But I'll have to hurry back before Snowy gets home and that's what's annoying me. I just want to do what I want.

Snowy sighs and deposits the basket on the landing. "Rapunzel, I realize seeing another person must have made you... curious. But you need to stay here."

"That's not fair."

"You think that because you don't know what it's like out there."

"That is your fault!" I say, my voice rising. I walk a few steps toward her. "You raised me to know nothing! And then you use that against me! Just how long do you think you can keep me up here?"

"Until it's safe again." She's still on the second step down from the landing. I give her a withering look. "How bad can it really be? You come and go every day without a scratch."

"I have magic to protect me."

"Do you use it?"

Snowy hesitates. I knew it.

"You don't! So, it's not dangerous all the time. You're just trying to scare me!"

"The Beast is real, Rapunzel. Almost two dozen girls have died. Do you want to be the next?"

"Have you seen the Beast yourself? How do we know it's not just a story?"

"I've seen tracks," Snowy says. "And the marks of claws on the trees. It's definitely a huge animal. A huge, savage, bloodthirsty animal."

"But why would the queen allow this?"

"She wants it! I told you that!"

"I was talking about you."

That gets her. She stares, blank and frozen.

"You...are...the queen," I say, dropping words like bass notes, heavy and strong. "And as queen, it is your duty to protect this kingdom. If a vicious animal is killing young girls, then *you* should be the one to hunt it down. If your throne has been stolen by some crazy witch lady, then *you* should be the one to drive her out. It's time you started acting like a queen, Snow White. It's who you are."

"You sound like my *mother*," she says. But her mask has momentarily crumbled. She looks no older than me at this moment, a little girl wounded and sad. It's a shame her own tears aren't magical because I see them shining in her eyes.

"If I don't want to be the queen, I don't have to be," she says in a shaky voice.

I cock my head. "Would Hunter be proud of that?"

Snowy drops to sit on the landing, covers her face, and starts crying. Good. Very good. At least we're getting somewhere.

"You don't understand!" she sobs.

"No, I think I do. It's all about Hunter, isn't it? That's why we're here. You wrapped your entire life around one stupid man. And when that man was taken away, you gave up! You ran away from your life because *he* wasn't in it anymore."

"That's not the whole story!" she shouts. "I lost your sister the same day. I was scared! I didn't want to lose you too!" She gives me a wet glare, like that doesn't sound so bad right now.

I'm too angry to feel sorry for her. "I know it was bad. But you should've gotten over it. I lost my childhood because of you. And I can never get that back!"

"You don't UNDERSTAND!" Snowy shrieks and she thrusts out her hand. Before I can think, something wet and piercing cold strikes my chest. I'm thrown high, off my feet, and hit the pipes of my organ. But I don't fall because the ice freezes thick around my body, trapping me there.

Chapter 10

I sleep in the kitchen on a folded blanket. The floor pokes the corners of my bones. I curl my body against the wall and hug my hair for comfort.

She never did that before. Attacked me with her magic. It didn't last long. After a minute, she felt guilty and drew the ice away and I crashed onto the keys of my organ, pipes moaning. My skin burned with frostbite and I was frozen straight through. I grabbed my braid and ran down the stairs to the kitchen. When Snowy tried to speak to me, I screamed and threw the kettle at her.

Next morning, she presents me with a new pair of socks, bright blue. She must've spent all night knitting them. "I've noticed your socks have grown thin," she says, kneeling beside my blanket.

It's an apology. I sit up and grudgingly take the socks. "Shoes would be better," I mumble. I don't have shoes because I never go out. Just socks for me, or when it's really cold, two pairs of socks.

"Would you like a pair of shoes?" Snowy asks, still trying to appease me. "I could buy you some slippers."

"No, I want to wear boots. Your boots. Just for today." I'm acting sulky but actually I just had a brilliant idea.

Snowy looks relieved. "That's fine. You can wear my boots today."

"And – and I want a new dress. Apple green," I say. "It's almost my birthday, anyway."

"Of course! I'll order one from the dressmaker, it should be done in time for your birthday. You said green?"

"Yeah. Could you go today? And could you get me some gingerbread? And a new book?" I know I sound too eager but I have to take advantage of her guilt as long as it lasts. I need her to leave the tower for a long time.

Snowy frowns. "But my boots...."

I scowl.

"Never mind. I'll wear my loafers," Snowy says. "But I did want to do the washing today."

"So? You can wash tomorrow. It's not as if we're expecting guests. And didn't you want to see that Wurley guy?"

Snowy looks annoyed. In any other circumstance, I know we'd be having a fight. She doesn't want to go out. But her guilt is still fresh and she can't afford to keep me angry. I don't cry magic tears when I'm angry.

So she goes.

And thankfully, Kay doesn't keep me waiting this time. Snowy's been gone only ten minutes when I hear his voice.

"Kay!" I glance at the cave and hush my voice. "She just left."

"I know," he says. He's wearing his thick black cloak as usual, but not the fur hat today. His dark hair looks slightly rustled. "I was lurking in the treetops. It's pretty impressive, the way the ice just opens up for her and falls back into place."

"She attacked me last night," I say. "She stuck me against the wall with her ice."

Kay loses his smile. "Well then. It's time to get you out of there." He's got a basket on the ground beside him, a wide one with a handle. A thick coil of rope lies inside it. "It's a little dirty, I got it from the stables. But it'll do the job." Kay grins as he unwinds the rope. "Now back up! I'm going to have to throw this."

I take five or six steps back from the window and my feet feel clunky in Snowy's boots. They fit well but I'm not used to them. I was smart enough to get dressed while I waited for Kay. I've got on my favorite warm blue dress and my brown bear cloak. I think I'm ready.

After a number of thuds against the outer wall, the rock soars through the window and hits the floor. It's slightly larger than my foot. The rope has been wrapped and knotted around it.

"Come back to the window!" Kay shouts.

"Do you want me to tie it somewhere?" I ask.

"No. Just drape it over the hook and let it hang. I'm going to lower you, much like the way you lower your sister. You'll have to trust me, all right?"

I nod. He instructs me to lower the rock until it's below the bottom edge of the window.

"Now sit on the sill and put your feet out," he says.

I climb carefully onto the ledge, cold air pouring over me, and my stomach feels like a ball of ice. It has just dawned on me that this window is really high.

Kay stands below me, holding the other end of the rope. "Put your feet on the rock and hold tight! I promise to do this slowly."

Awkwardly, I pinch the rock with my boots and curl my fingers around the rope. But my bottom stays firmly stuck to the sill. Oh my blood and bones! The ground looks miles away. I can't just push off and dangle with all that air underneath me. How does Snowy do this?

"Close your eyes," Kay says.

No, not seeing is far worse. So, I clench my teeth, squeeze the rope, and ungracefully slide my rear off the sill. And now I'm floating, swaying, twirling slowly. I grip the rope with my hands, elbows, and thighs, my feet tilted onto the rock. Kay begins to lower me and although he's careful, it's a series of small, gut-stabbing drops. I hold my breath and watch the ground come closer, bit by awful bit. And finally, the rock touches dirt.

"Oh!" I step onto the earth and bend over, hands on my wobbly knees. "Oh, that was so much worse than I thought it would be!"

Kay laughs. "Your hair!"

I look back. My braid swoops up to the window, five floors above, the end of it still in the tower. Laughing, I give a tug and it falls, rustling, into a heap behind me.

Kay hands me the basket. "You can use this to carry it."

"Thank you." I take the basket but I'm staring at Kay's face. It's my first time seeing him up close. He's got pleasant brown eyes and black lashes. His nose is wider than mine and his jaw looks squarish. He has black hair, cut short around the sides of his head, but longer and denser on top. He's a lot taller than me and has a sturdy look about him. I think he's impressive.

Kay grins at me with his shiny, white teeth. "Hello, Rapunzel. Welcome to the world."

Chapter II

The first part is hardest. Getting down the hill. We can't go through the cave, not with the entrance all clogged up with Snowy's ice. Kay shows me how he comes and goes, climbing a slope that feels more like the side of a cliff by gripping the shrubs that grow there. Going down is slow, scary work and the basket hooked on my elbow throws my weight off balance. I slip and skid a few times, smearing dirt up my side, before Kay catches hold of my arm. It's as bad, possibly worse, than going out the window. Because it takes much longer.

We work our way down three sections of hillside. And then, Kay says, we're on the forest floor. I'm in The Wood now.

I look up... and love it all. The trees, the leaves, the bits of sky between them. Trunks in shades of brown or gray - the tall, slender ones with papery bark, the stout, twisted ones with harsh ridges. I spot a squirrel and watch it skitter from one branch to another and my heart cramps up at how beautiful it is.

I let my eyes wander, pulling it all in, aware that Kay remains quiet. He's letting me look. After a few minutes, I sigh and smile at him. "All right."

"Ready?" Kay guides me to a path between the trees. I fall in step beside him. Our path is spotted with lumps of snow and puddles of dark water. It all smells soggy and cold. I can't believe I'm out of my tower. I can't believe I'm going somewhere.

"So, we're going to a village?" I ask.

Kay winces. "I did promise you that. But there's a problem."

"What is it?"

"There's to be a celebration at the palace today. When I spoke to you yesterday, I honestly forgot all about it. And I'm expected to be there. Believe me, I wanted to kick myself this morning when my mother reminded me. But – if you want – you could go there with me. Would you like to?"

"A celebration?" I stare at him in wonder. "Do you mean it's like... a party?"

Kay laughs. "Oh yes. Quite a big one. The queen had her first child last month. Hence the festivities. She's invited everyone to see the baby. You wanted to see people, didn't you?"

"Yes. Yes, I do." But now I'm confused. "Kay... how can this be the queen's first child? I thought *you* were the first child."

"The queen isn't my mother. She's my aunt."

"But you're still a prince?"

"So they tell me!" Kay grins.

"But the queen - isn't she cruel and horrible? Snowy says she is."

Kay smirks. "She got a nasty temper, that's for sure. Does an awful lot of yelling. Personally, I just stay away from her. She doesn't like to be argued with, even a little."

"And what about the Beast?"

"You know about the Beast?" Kay looks shocked.

"Of course. I know it does the queen's bidding and she's using it to kill young girls."

"Whoa, wait. Hang on a second." Kay stops and takes hold of my shoulder. "Yes, there is a Beast. Yes, it has been killing young girls. But no, it's not doing the queen's bidding. She wouldn't do that."

"Then where'd it come from?"

"We think from another kingdom. No one's seen it here before. The queen has her best huntsmen tracking it down but they haven't found it yet. It never comes out in daylight."

"Daylight." I look at the sky, reassuringly blue. "So, we're safe now?"

Kay grins. "Safe from the Beast. But beware of humans."

We continue on our path and I see wonderful things. Things that, until now, I've only read about in books. A stream that cuts through the forest floor, clear and sparkling. A deer picking through the snow on thin, graceful legs. Chipmunks that dart out from under logs, startling me.

"Look! Look at that!" I point at a spider web that stretches between two trees. The frost has coated each delicate strand so they look like threads of silver. I press a hand to my chest. "That is the most beautiful thing I have ever seen."

"That?" Kay looks doubtful.

"You don't think so?"

He shrugs. "It's pretty."

I give him a scowl. "Not good enough for you? Fine. What's *your* most beautiful thing in the world?"

Kay looks at the ground. His cheeks redden, a startling shade in this drab and colorless forest. "A – a girl."

"A girl?" I don't believe it. More beautiful than a frozen spider web?

Kay lets out a long sigh, whitening the air. "There's a girl that I... like very much. She is absolutely perfect, the most beautiful creature alive. It hurts my heart just to look at her."

"Why?"

"Because she takes no notice of me. I am but one admirer of the many that she has. I can't even speak to her that much, I see her only at balls and parties where she's always surrounded by people."

"She has a lot of friends?"

"Oh yes, she's quite popular. There's something irresistible about her, she...." He looks at me as if suddenly worried. "I'm sorry."

"For what?"

"For bringing her up. Perhaps you don't know about things like this."

"Of course, I do. You're in love with her."

Kay's cheeks glow redder. "I'm sorry, I shouldn't have said anything. In my experience, I've found that girls don't like it when you mention other girls. They get mad."

"I'm not mad." But something's bugging me, I can feel it. Barely there but enough to bother me, like an almost headache.

"Oh good," Kay says, relieved. "I don't want to offend you, you've been nice. You're a good friend."

My heart rips open at his words. That's what it feels like - a hot, blazing plain that splits my chest. "Really?" I lunge and grip the side of his cloak. "Do you mean it? Are we really friends?"

Kay grins. "Sure! Sure we are." His eyes soften as he looks at me. "You're not used to having one. I get it."

"Yeah, I'm really – I'm really glad about this, Kay. I – I hope we can do lots of stuff together. I hope – I hope this other girl won't...."

"No, she won't. Even if I marry her, you and I will still be friends." He smiles but another sigh escapes him. "But that's never going to happen. She doesn't want me, I don't impress her."

"But you're the prince. Shouldn't that impress her a little bit?"

"Just the opposite. She thinks it means I do nothing worthwhile, that I've had an easy life and never had to work for anything. She'll have nothing to do with me unless I do something heroic."

I scowl. "She doesn't sound very nice."

"When she wants to be, she's the sweetest girl in the world. I'm determined...." He rakes back his hair with fingers. "I'm determined, Rapunzel. I have to win over this girl. My Beauty."

Chapter 12

Even her name is Beauty. That's so dumb. Two minutes ago, I didn't know this girl existed. And I already hate her. Despite Kay's assurances, I know she's going to be a problem.

My feet are getting tired in Snowy's boots. I'm not used to walking this much. And I've never had to carry my hair for so long, the basket is heavy on my arm and switching to the other for relief isn't helping.

"I need to sit down."

"Now?" Kay says. "I don't mean to rush you, but we need to hurry if we want to make the party."

"I'm tired." I find a large rock only partly covered in snow and brush it off with a corner of my cloak. "I want some water."

"Sure. That stream we saw isn't too far back."

"Good." I sit on the rock. "I'll wait here."

Kay gives me a puzzled look. "Did I say I was getting it for you?"

"Well, how else am I supposed to get it?"

Kay smirks. "I don't fetch water. I'm a prince."

"Neither do I. I'm a princess."

Kay cocks an eyebrow. "Since when?"

"Since always." I pull my braid into my lap and smooth it with my hand. "I've been denied my rightful inheritance."

Kay opens his mouth to argue and then groans. "I guess that's... kind of true. All right, Princess Rapunzel, just this once. I can't afford to waste time." He steps off the trail into The Wood and points at me. "But stay there! Don't wander off for any reason."

"I won't."

I cover my legs with the brown bear cloak and lift the hood. I can feel the coolness of the rock seeping through, but otherwise, the cloak keeps me warm. I smile and let myself enjoy my few minutes alone. I still can't believe I'm out here, out of my tower. I know I'll have to get home before Snowy returns tonight. This is only my first escape and I want to have more - until I think of a way to leave the tower for good.

The Wood looks enormous, like it has no end. I'm so used to seeing it from the window, the same angle, the same view. I study the trees close to me, the patterns of their bark. I scrape the ground with my boot and listen to the scratchy sound it makes. I break a small branch off a bush beside me and turn it over in my fingers, studying how the leaves connect to the branch.

From the left, I hear footsteps coming toward me, squashing the snow. I look up, expecting Kay – but it's not Kay at all.

It's a huge, huge man.

Chapter 13

I can't do anything but stare. The man is enormous, at least seven feet tall. I didn't know people could get that big.

"Lose your way, little miss?" he asks. His voice scares me to death. Rough and resonant, like I mashed down all the low keys of my organ at once. He's got scruffy hair and a long beard, a mixture of black and gray. My nose fills with the smell of him, wood smoke and stewed beef and the mustiness of unwashed hair. I'm repulsed and fascinated all at once.

"Where you headed?" he asks.

My throat is tight, I can't say a thing. This huge man seems to fill my whole world. He wears an open leather vest over loose clothing, with no cloak to keep out the cold. There's an axe on his shoulder and the hand that grips it has only three fingers. I want Kay to come back, right now, right now! I want to go back to my tower.

The man looks around. "You shouldn't be out here alone. Not safe. Are you from one of the villages?"

I look down and shake my head. If I don't talk, maybe he'll just go away.

The man exhales and drops the axe from his shoulder. "Look, missy. I don't know how you got here, but I'm taking you to the nearest village. This part of The Wood is dangerous, especially for girls. Come with me." He bends and grabs my upper arm with his huge, three-fingered hand, and fear, wild fear, explodes inside my head. The trees blur together, turn gray and then black.

∎∎

I open my eyes. I'm staring at a ceiling, crossed by heavy beams. There are cobwebs between them, which annoys me. Snowy really should've cleaned those away.

I turn my head – and realize I'm not at home. I'm lying on a bed, on a quilt made of squares. The whole room is a square, so unlike my round tower. The walls are made of wood instead of stone. There's a window on my right and through it I see the gray trunks of trees.

I'm still in The Wood.

Slowly, I push myself up. My braid hangs off the bed and falls into the basket, although some of it has spilled out. I ease off the bed and crouch, my hands shaking as I scoop the hair into the basket. He can't be far - the room is full of his smell. And something else, strong and musky, that makes me wrinkle my nose. I need to leave here as fast as I can.

The door to my room hangs open. I listen and hear creaking on the floorboards above me, the sound of a heavy tread. He's upstairs. I stand, clutching the handle of my basket and creep into the next room. It's all wood, like the last one, except for a stone fireplace. There's a table with a large rocking chair beside it, a shelf that holds a few dishes, a floor in desperate need of sweeping. And, best of all, a door that goes outside.

"Oh, you're up," says a voice and I nearly jump out of my boots. The huge man is sitting on a staircase by the left-hand wall. I was looking at the door and didn't notice. He's got an apple in his hands and is peeling off the skin with a small knife. How did he get down here so fast?

"Look, don't pass out again," he says. "I didn't mean to scare you, I was trying to be a friend."

A friend?

The man indicates the door with his knife. "Go on. You shouldn't be here but I didn't know what else to do. Couldn't show up at some village with you passed out, they'd think I attacked you. Couldn't leave you to freeze in The Wood either. Just go back where you came from and do it quick, all right?"

I nod. The floor above me creaks again and I glance up at the ceiling. Is there...?

"You understand, girl?" the man barks. "Or are you soft in the head?"

"I understand." I'm less afraid since he said he was a friend. I didn't know friends could look – and smell - that unpleasant. But if that's what he is, it means he won't hurt me.

I clear my throat. "I don't know where to go."

"What?"

"I was on my way to the palace. I need to know how to get back there."

"The palace?" The man looks at my dress and then my boots.

"Yes, I was going there with my friend Kay."

"Kay? Kay who?" the man asks sharply.

"Kay who lives at the palace."

The man spits out a harsh word I never heard before. "Why didn't you tell me you were with the prince? I thought you were alone!"

"He was getting me some water."

The man exhales loudly. "Could've just told me that instead of acting like a shivering pup. He's probably wandering around out there looking for you."

"Well, it's not my fault. You looked dangerous!"

"Naw, not anymore. Too old for that stuff. Look, wait for me outside, all right? I'll take you back to Kay."

"Could I have some water first?"

The man bites into his apple and glares at me. "There's a well out back. Help yourself."

I nod, although I really think he should bring it to me. But I'm still a little bit scared of him, so I shut my mouth and go outside.

I walk down a short path made of broad, flat stones. At the end of it, I turn and look back.

Oh - it's a cottage! I was in a cottage! It's the cutest thing I ever saw, with a pointed roof covered in snow, a crooked chimney, and stone walls with little pockets of windows. I always heard cottages were small but this one looks quite big to me. I bet it has more rooms than my tower.

But I don't see a well and I'm really thirsty now. He said out back. What does out back mean? Does it mean behind the cottage?

It's not easy to walk around the house. The ground along the sides is all bushes and weeds and a broken wheelbarrow blocks my way. The snow is lumpy with rocks and random bits of rubbish - my new friend is not very tidy.

There's a flat area behind the cottage, a sort of rectangular clearing. I guess this is out back. Like everything else, it's frosted in snow and the trees of The Wood stand around it. I don't see a well – but I'm not looking for it. Something else has caught my attention.

A strange box stands in the middle of the yard. A box made of glass with long silver legs. I can't see much of it – it's all under snow – but it looks very fancy and shiny. Certainly an odd thing to keep out back.

I've spotted the well at the corner of the yard, so I shrug off the strange box and head over there. But I can't help glancing over my shoulder. On the other side of the box, there's a section of glass where the snow has blown away. And I can see something inside it.

I stop hard, my eyes widening.

It's a hand.

Chapter 14

My stomach twists inside me. I back away, not believing, but I keep on looking. There's a hand in there. A hand resting on dark fabric. Could it be... is there really... a *person* in there?

My breath comes out in puffs of white. I want to run away but I have to figure this out. With the basket hooked on my arm, I scavenge around the yard until I find a long stick. After edging as close to the box as I dare, I reach out and scrape the snow off the end of it. Oh my blood and bones. Small feet in pointy shoes. Black fabric that rests loosely over the ankles, like a skirt. If there's a person in there, it's a girl person.

That part makes me slightly braver. I drop the stick and walk to the opposite end of the box. I lift my hand and let it hover over the lid. I hope I won't regret this. I just want to see what it is.

I place my hand on the cold glass and sweep the snow aside. It's wet but slides off almost clean. I pause, breathless, and stare through the glass.

It's a lady. A lady with yellow hair. I have never seen real yellow hair before and it's lovelier than I imagined. Bright as gold, soft as air, it curves with her face and lies smoothly on her shoulders. She's sleeping - I think. I mean, she can't be dead, right? Her cheeks are fresh and pink. I don't know why she'd want to sleep out here, in a box, in the cold. But she's lovely. I feel a strange kind of peacefulness just looking at her. I like her dark, curling lashes. And the arc of her eyebrows. And her little mouth, pointy and proud. I can't tell her age, but she's older than me. Maybe like Snowy.

I realize I've been holding my breath and release a sigh. I brush away more snow, ignoring the tingle in my fingers. The lady wears a black dress, cut well for her slim figure. It's dark and yet it shines. With this, I also notice the black tiara in her hair - a spray of dark, metal branches with black crystals at their tips. It looks amazing in her golden hair. I don't know who she is but I can feel she's special. Maybe she's a fairy and this is how they sleep.

"Get away from there!"

I leap back, terrified. The big man has emerged. He stands next to the cottage and glares at me. The axe is parked on his shoulder again.

"You scared me!" I shout at him.

"Get over here now," he growls.

"Who's this lady?"

"Leave her be."

"But who is she? Why is she sleeping in a box?"

"She cursed. Let's go."

"She's cursed?"

"Did you get your water?"

"No, not yet, but-"

"GET IT NOW!" The man points at the well, face like a furnace.

I get my water.

But I'm not done with this. I wait until we're back on the trail and the red flames have cooled from his cheeks. It's not just curiosity, I feel sad for this lady. I want to know.

"If you please... can you tell me more about the lady? And why she was cursed?"

"She's the Cursed Queen. Thought you kids were taught about her by your folks. She was queen of our land for a while but now she sleeps. Not likely to ever wake up."

My heart sinks within me. "Who did that to her?"

"Look – when you get back home, get someone to tell you about her. I don't have time for it. I keep her safe from prying eyes and poking fingers. That's all."

"That's all you do?"

He groans. "That's all you want to know about."

I look ahead at the trail, the twisted roots that run across it, the trampled snow, the trees with their sad, sagging leaves. And back at the man. "Is this about the noise I heard upstairs?"

"Keep quiet."

"No. I don't like your attitude."

This brings out a harsh, gravelly laugh from the man. He lifts a hand and shows me the back of it. "You won't like this across your face either, missy. Now shut it."

"You said we were friends."

"We're not friends."

"Why not?"

"I know nothing about you. Other than you're insane to grow your hair that long. I'm beginning to think you escaped from some place."

"I did. I escaped from my tower. My sister is the Snow Queen and if she learned you mistreated me she would kill you in an instant!"

There's a shift in the man's eyebrows and his heavy gait slows for a moment. "Snow White."

"You know her?"

The man looks at me. There's a deep crease between his eyebrows and frown lines around his mouth. "You survived?"

"What are you talking about?"

"We didn't think the babies survived. They lost their mother."

"No, I'm – I'm fine."

"And the other one?"

"She was stolen from us. I don't know where she is. But... but how do you know about it?"

"I was there the day Snowy ran away."

I'm beginning to understand something. The stories Snowy has told me a hundred times are becoming real. "Are you... a Dwarf?"

The man smirks and holds out a hand. "Barker. At your service, miss."

That does it.

I run.

Chapter 15

But I don't get far. Within two bounds, the man reaches me and jerks me back by the arm. "If I was going to harm you, I'd have done it by now, don't you think?" he shouts.

"Let me go!"

"Not until I've brought you to Kay. Now stop your fussing or I'll put you over my shoulder again. ENOUGH!"

I stop my fussing. There's nothing I can do, he's too big. "You're as horrible as Snowy said you all were."

"Yeah? Her hands aren't squeaky clean either. She tell you about Hunter?"

"Oh yes."

"What's she got to say about it?"

I sigh. "She misses him. More than anything."

"Anything else?"

"She says his death froze her heart. And that's why the kingdom is cold."

Barker's eyebrows drop lower but not in an angry way. "She's been away too long. She should come back."

"Why?"

"RAPUNZEL!"

Oh, thanks be to everything, I hear Kay. "Over here!" I call out. I turn to the section of The Wood from where I heard his voice and moments later, Kay comes dashing out from the trees. "There you are! What happened?" He looks as pale as Snowy. And surprised to see the Dwarf. "Barker!"

"Sorry, Kay. The girl lost her wits and I had to take her to the cottage. She's all right now."

"I've been looking for an hour!" Kay's voice is hoarse. "I thought something terrible had happened, she was nowhere! We're supposed to be at the palace!"

"Well, take her and go, she's caused me enough trouble. That family always does." The man nudges me with his huge hand. "Look here. When you see Snowy next, tell her Barker says hello. Tell her we wouldn't mind it if she came back to us. We're not mad now, it all worked out."

I nod. "All right." The man heads away from us, the blade of the axe peeking over his shoulder. Kay pulls me in the opposite direction and we return to our original trail. We've been set back a bit, he tells me. His voice his strained for a while, he runs his fingers through his hair and blows the air from his cheeks several times.

"I'm sorry," he says after we've walked in silence for twenty minutes. "I'm just a little... but we'll be fine. We'll be late for the celebration but the beginning is boring anyway. Introductions and speeches and stuff. I just hope we get there in time for the ceremonies. The queen will be mad if I miss that."

"Remember, I have to get home before Snowy."

"Sure." Kay's smile is beginning to grow back. "I've got to tell you, that was rough when I was looking for you. You don't have the easiest name to yell. 'RaPUNzel! RaPUNzel!' I shouted – but not too loud. I was afraid the Snow Queen might hear me.

"Oh!" Impulsively, I check over shoulder. "She must be far away by now."

"Well, with that in mind, in the *unlikely* event that I misplace you again, I'm thinking a nickname might be useful."

"I don't have a nickname."

"Fortunately, it's not hard to make one up. I've been thinking about this for several minutes. True enough, your name doesn't lend itself easily to nicknaming. So, I've broken it down into three parts: Rap, Pun, and Zel, and tried each one. Now Rappy doesn't work well at all, I think."

"Oh gobs, no." I wrinkle my nose.

"And Punzy sounds like an old man with a big stomach."

I burst into surprised laughter and it's the best feeling in the world. "That's even worse!"

"So, what about Zelly?"

"Zelly?"

"Yeah. It's cute, and it fits you." He smiles, the one I like that makes me happy inside.

I smile back. "Acceptable."

Chapter 16

"Dark days. Dark days. That's all she talks about. Her excuse for keeping me locked up."

Kay frowns. "She sounds afraid. Has she been hurt by someone?"

I sigh. "She does talk about... things."

"But is she cruel? Does she really murder anyone who tries to speak to her? Is her skin blue?"

"What?"

Kay grins and pushes back a stray branch that hangs in our path. "I know, another myth. I grew up hearing about the Ice Witch. She was spoken of like an evil spirit, not an actual person. Whenever it snowed, someone said the Ice Witch was angry. It killed all the farms, the peasants were starving. Many people left the kingdom."

"Really?"

"No one likes an endless winter. Most of the villages are now abandoned and sit there rotting. But the towns are still populated. I'm told there's been a near-complete turnover of the people since the days when Edgar was king. A few old families have remained out of loyalty. The rest are refugees from war-torn kingdoms, or people who don't mind spending their lives indoors, or have businesses that agree with cold weather. Furriers are doing well."

My mouth falls open. "So, these 'dark days' that Snowy *loves* to talk about... are actually her doing! It's her fault!" Oh, this is glorious. What a weapon I have. "But never mind, tell me more."

"You hungry?"

"Not yet."

"Well, naturally, there was a lot of speculation about the Ice Witch. Who she was, where she was.... A group of men swore up and down that she was the former princess, Snow White. But most people didn't believe them. Snow White was described as unremarkable, certainly not magical. And the men were criminals."

"The Dwarves?"

"You know about the Dwarves?" Kay cries.

"Of course. They were a gang of criminals. I didn't realize that big man was one of them until a few minutes ago."

"Yeah, that was Barker. The rest have married, they're no longer a gang. Actually, the oldest one-"

"So, who did you think the Snow Queen was? If she wasn't Snow White?"

"Most people thought she was some kind of witch who got banished from her kingdom and was taking it out on us. We weren't sure, we just wanted the winter to stop. But nobody knew where she lived."

I can't help but feel smug. Snowy always said our tower is well hidden. Although it's built on a high ledge, it can't be seen from The Wood below. Somehow the trees block the view.

"But... Snowy goes out almost every day," I say. "Hasn't anyone recognized her?"

"Maybe. Like I said, there's been a turnover in the population. She must have a story ready in case someone does ask. But one secret she has kept very well: no one knows she's the Ice Witch."

"The *Snow Queen*," I say.

"Whatever you want! Some people call her the Frost Demon. She's a problem that everyone talks about and nobody wants to face. Believe me, it's been a headache to the real queen for ages."

"Snowy *is* the real queen," I say.

"I would argue with that. She abandoned the palace and shows no interest in her people. The throne was up for grabs. Snow White couldn't have it now."

"She could if she wanted! She can do anything with her magic."

"Yet she chooses to hide away in the hills and throw snowflakes around." Kay looks at me and raises one of his long black eyebrows.

I should be mad at him. I kind of am. But he's only saying what I've said to Snowy for years. And Kay doesn't look mad, more like he's teasing.

I shrug. "Well... I guess she likes doing things her own way."

Kay's eyes travel from my head down to the hair in my basket. "You don't say?"

I roll my eyes. He does an odd flinch and stares at me.

"What?" I say.

"Sorry. You roll your eyes just like Beauty does. She does it the same way, rolls and blinks twice."

"She does it to you?"

"All the time."

"Why?"

"I don't know. I don't impress her." He gives a light-hearted laugh but I can see he's bothered by it. "She says I have no achievements. I'm not a hero, I haven't won a battle or sacrificed myself to save another. She says she could only love a man she admires."

I scowl. "That doesn't sound right. I mean...." I'm not sure how to explain it. "She says you have to be a hero. But what about her? What makes her deserve that? If you have to be a hero than she has to be special too!"

"Oh, she's special. She's more beautiful than the fairies. My heart burns whenever I think of her. I'd walk a hundred miles just to kiss the smallest finger of her hand. I – I don't know what to do, Zelly."

I release a silent sigh. This sounds like Snowy and her Hunter. Love is so dumb. But I'll humor him for now, after all, he's my friend. "Well, let's think about it. You need to do something she'd consider heroic. Is there anything she likes?"

"Flowers. Gardens. She loves the rose garden at the palace because she can't have one of her own. It's too cold. Our garden never freezes, oddly enough."

"Hmm. I'm not sure that helps us. Is she afraid of anything?"

Kay nods. "The Beast. She is very much afraid of the Beast. But then, so are all the girls."

"Well, that's easy. Kill the Beast."

Kay jumps. "What?"

"That would make you a hero. Definitely."

"I can't kill the Beast!" Kay laughs. "I've never even seen it! I wouldn't know where to look!"

"So? Hunt for it! You'd be doing the kingdom a favor."

"I've never even killed a rabbit."

"I'm just *saying*, Prince Kay, that this is something that might impress your little Beauty." The beginning of a scheme is forming in my head. It's not nice – but Snowy never taught me to be nice. Two things seem to be threatening the new life I'm starting: Beauty... and the Beast. I think I can use Kay to get rid of the Beast.

And then I'll get rid of Beauty.

Chapter 17

I don't know what I was expecting. But not this. The trees just *end*. They were all around us, snug and quiet. But I picked up new smells, felt a breeze on my face. And then we reached the end of The Wood. I have never seen land without trees.

It's flat and uncovered. A field of snow so white, I find myself blinking. A few scraggly, black bushes reach out like boney hands and there are two narrow grooves that cut through the snow and curl with the land. At the back of it all is the palace.

"It's so... big!" I say. All my life, I've seen the palace from my tower. Just a pretty little toy down in the valley. Now I'm gazing upward, stunned at how it stands above the world, solid and beautiful. It's got a large, squarish midsection with towers that seem to grow from the walls and climb to the sky. So many towers! All of them bigger than mine. I can't believe that people, puny little people, could build something like this.

We don't talk much as we cross the field. Kay guides me into one of the long grooves, which he explains were made by carriage wheels. I walk in one groove, he in the other, about six feet apart. I can't stop gawking at the palace.

"What do you do with all those rooms?" I ask.

"Anything you want! We've got a room just for sitting and thinking. Doesn't get used much."

"How did they get the towers up there?"

"Honestly, I have no idea."

"What's under my feet?"

"Gravel," Kay says. "We're on the main drive up to the palace. It's always under snow, they gave up trying to keep it clear."

The palace creeps closer and our grooves bend to face the front of it. My eyes widen. "Look at the stairs!" At home, the stairs follow the curling wall of the tower, but the edge of each step is straight. Here, the steps – must be forty or fifty of them – go straight up to the doors but their edges curve back. Steps like circles. Doors like giants. On the wall far above, a large clock with gold numbers. I think I like this palace.

"Shall we?" Kay smiles and points his elbow at me. I stare, bewildered, until I figure out that he wants me to hold the inside of his arm. As we climb the stairs, my stomach gets all jumpy and wriggly. "Do I look the way I should? I know people like to make themselves fancy for a party."

"Your dress is fine," Kay says. "And don't worry about the boots, you needed them to get here. I'll ask my mother to find you some dancing slippers."

The doors are opened by two strange men, very stiff and serious. I give them a curious glance but they don't even look at us. Kay instructs me to give them my bear cloak. "And leave the basket. Outrageous hair is common at a party."

"Oh... all right." I'm feeling uncomfortable. But I set the basket on the floor and gather up my braid. I sometimes do this at home when I'm tired of my hair, I hang it in long hoops from my arms, like a shawl. It's heavy but it keeps it off the floor.

"Perfect!" Kay says. "You'll fit right in." He takes me down a corridor with shiny walls and through another set of doors. We're standing at the top of a staircase again, in a room of white and gold. I'm seeing so many things I've only read about in books: chandeliers that look like sparkly trees hanging upside down; a marble floor with swirls of white and gray that holds the light inside it; columns bearing up the ceiling where a blue sky and angels have been painted above our heads. And best of all, far better than anything else – I see people. Lots and lots of people.

Silently, we slip down the stairs. Kay smiles with ease but I clench him arm, afraid. My ears are crowded with too many sounds - music, voices, laughter. The people shift and flow around each other. The ladies' dresses stand out to me, each one a different color. Like bright triangles, I think. And the men look like dark lines between them. I'm seeing so many new things, it's almost too much. I drop my eyes to the stairs to rest them.

"We're in luck!" Kay says. "We missed the talks and the dancing but not the dinner. That should be next. Are you hungry?"

I nod. Actually, I'm very hungry. And I think I smell pork, which Snowy almost never buys for me. But I don't want to eat here, it's too shiny and loud. I need a place where I can close my eyes and breathe until I'm ready to face it again.

Kay tugs my arm. "Come with me."

"Are we going to eat?"

"Not yet. I'm taking you to meet the queen."

Chapter 18

Oh sugar. Oh snap. Kay pulls me through all those lines and triangles while I try not to look afraid. It feels like a very long room. He leads me to the other side, right up to the wall. There are two chairs sitting under a canopy and a curtain that falls behind them. I've never seen a curtain against a wall before-

"Rapunzel?"

"What?"

Kay lifts a hand. "The king and queen."

Oh. I should've been looking at the people. The two chairs hold a man and a woman, both of them staring at me. They are large people and their clothing is heavy and overdone. Especially on the woman. She just takes up too much space, her dress is nothing but puffs and ruffles in a shocking shade of purple. She looks like fabric exploded.

I turn to Kay. "*That's* the queen?"

Kay stiffens. The queen, who was frowning before, frowns harder. "Kay, what is this?"

"Uh, Aunt Lunilla, this is my friend, Lady Rapunzel. Rapunzel, this is Queen Lunilla."

I don't like her. Don't like her hard, square face and heavy cheeks. Or her red hair, even brighter than mine, all fussed up and curled in odd places. I can only describe her as glamorously ugly. An attack on the eyes.

"Where's your curtsy, child?" Lunilla asks.

Sugar. I don't know how to curtsy. And I don't really see why I should before this mess. So I shrug.

"Did you bring me an idiot, Kay?" Lunilla asks. Her eyes drop to my boots. "Or a country peasant?"

"Oh no! No, no, no, Aunt Lunilla. Pardon my friend, she... she has been ill. For a long time. She may have forgotten-"

"She looks familiar." Lunilla squints her eyes at me. "Do I know your family, Runzel?"

"Rapunzel. No."

"Hmm... your face annoys me, though. Like I've seen it before. Turn your head! Let me see your profile."

I don't like the bossy way she talks. So I don't turn my head. Kay shifts his weight toward me and whispers, "Please." Oh fine, I'll do it for him. I turn my chin to my left shoulder.

"Look at her, Cooper. Does she look familiar to you?" Lunilla asks.

Now, I notice the king. And at first, I think it's Barker from The Wood. Huge and hairy, like him. But this man is slightly different. His beard is a faded shade of brown and looks combed. He has all ten of his fingers. And better clothes.

"I don't know her," he says gruffly.

"She doesn't live nearby." Kay says.

"Ill-bred, obviously. That hairpiece is absurd." Lunilla drops her eyes to the braid hanging from my arms. "Kay, why did you bring an ignorant country girl to our celebration?"

I feel hot all at once, scorching mad. "I am NOT an ignorant country girl. I am a princess! My mother was Cinderella, your former queen. So, do not mock me!"

Lunilla looks utterly frozen. Her heavy lips are parted as she gazes at me. "You... are Cinderella's daughter." She sounds amazed. "Why didn't I see it? She's right there in your face. And in your attitude." With a half-smile, her eyes slide to Kay. "Where did you find her?"

"I'll tell you later," Kay mutters. He doesn't look happy at all. "Listen, I'm sorry we're late. We had a long walk-"

"Nobody cares." She speaks to Kay but keeps her eyes on me. "Cindy's daughter, well, well, well. What a treasure. You must keep her with us, Kay, at the head table. She's a *royal* guest."

"Thank you, but...." Kay draws a deep breath. "I wasn't planning on putting her at the head table. She's been out of society for a long time and I thought a quiet corner would be better. I'll stay with her."

"I would much prefer that," I say. I don't understand the talk of head tables but I know what quiet corners are. I want to get away from this purple cow.

Lunilla puffs up like an angry bird. Before she can speak, the king cuts in. "Go ahead, Kay. We thought you weren't coming and gave your place to Prince Eric and his wife."

"We'll tell them to move," Lunilla says.

"That'll make a ruckus. Let's keep it nice, we don't want a lot of noise, upsetting the baby."

Lunilla scowls. "All right, fine, just for dinner. But don't go far, Runzel! I will speak to you later."

"Thank you." Kay bows and almost yanks me away. We cross the room again and I'm aware that people are looking at me. I don't like how it feels. I want to brush those strange eyes off my skin like spiders.

We don't go back to the stairs. In the middle of the room, Kay swerves to the left. The wall ahead is lined with huge mirrors and I'm startled when I see myself and Kay in them. I can't imagine why the mirrors are here. Does the queen get dressed in this big room?

Kay takes me to the last chair at the last table. We are literally in the corner, with the wall on two sides. But our chairs are facing outward, so I can watch what's going on. Kay sinks into the chair beside me and drops his head in his hands. "Oh Zelly."

"What's the matter?"

"I wish you hadn't told her that."

"Told her what?"

"Whose daughter you are. It's my fault, I should've warned you."

I'm startled by a blast of music and a loud voice announcing supper. The people break apart from each other and head for the tables. A few of them are coming our way. My hands start to tremble. I've never seen this many people before and I don't know what I should do.

Kay drops his voice low. "I didn't realize you were Cinderella's daughter. You didn't tell me."

"I told you I was Snowy's sister," I whisper. The people are getting into the chairs.

"Yes. But Snowy's mother wasn't Cinderella. I didn't make the connection. I should have. But I thought her children didn't survive."

"Well, I did. Is that a problem?"

"Yes," Kay says. "It means you have a claim to the throne and Aunt Lunilla won't like that. The people have pretty much accepted her as queen because they can't do much about it. But among those who have lived here for generations, there's a lot of debate about who rightfully should be in power. Most agree that Snow White is the rightful queen. But she ran away from it. Now you, as King Edgar's second daughter, have the strongest claim. You might not care about that but Aunt Lunilla will."

87

Oh, I care. I'm thrilled I have the strongest claim. I always knew I deserved to be the queen.

Kay says little more because the people arrive at our table. A lady in a yellow dress greets him in surprise and questions why he'd be at the bottom table. Kay laughs it off and introduces me and I give her a quiet smile. I have no idea what I should say.

A whole bunch of slim, serious men carry out plates of food and set them on the tables. I have read about feasts in my storybooks, about platters of food piled high. But to see it – meats and fruits and breads and cheeses stacked up like mountains is more wonderful than I imagined. It looks too beautiful to touch but everyone does.

The yellow lady likes talking to Kay and doesn't try to speak to me at all. Which is fine because I want to look at the people. I stuff my mouth with the best pork I ever had and just stare at them.

It's strange and fascinating and disturbing. So many different kinds of faces. At my table is a man who has bright green eyes that I find amazing and beautiful. And a lady with white hair and wrinkly skin that hangs very loose on her neck. A man with a large, bony nose who waves his hands a lot when he talks. A stout lady with two chins and breasts so large, they don't fully fit inside her dress. Everyone's skin is a slightly different shade, some as pale as Snowy, some reddish and rough, some dark brown and shiny. I notice my red hair color is not common. Other than the queen, there's only two other heads in the room like mine.

I crane my neck to look further out. That must be the head table near the top of the room. I see the king and queen and their friends, also overdressed and over-decorated. They sit on one side, looking out across the room, unlike our tables which have seats all around.

I shift my gaze to the next table near them, in the exact opposite corner from where I'm sitting. I gasp and grab Kay's arm, my eyes nearly jumping out of my head.

"Those are fairies!"

Chapter 19

I count them. Twelve fairies at the table. Sitting on chairs without backs, leaving their wings unhindered. Their dresses are simple and flowing, without sleeves, gathered by a cord at their waists. I can't tell what they're eating but each of them has a tiny gold plate.

"I want to see them closer!" I start to get up but Kay grabs my arm. "Not yet! Nobody can stand before the meal is over."

"I'm done!" I indicate my empty plate.

"The king and queen are not and that's all that matters. We have to stay put."

I sigh. More waiting. And it seems to take a very long time. I thought we had plenty of food on our tables but the slim, serious men take away the platters and bring back more. This time with cakes and pastries and pies. I secure a square of gingerbread but I'm too full to do more than nibble at the corners. The yellow lady decides to talk to me for a while, which I find more stressful than enjoyable.

At last, the platters are taken away. And I don't know how this happens, but everyone stands up at once, which confuses me. How do they know? What are we doing?

The people turn toward an open area near the center of the ballroom. A strange lady is pushing out a wooden box that stands on wheels. It's very shiny, with flowers cut into the wood, and one side of it has a little hooded canopy. She leaves it in the middle of the room.

"What's that?" I ask Kay.

"The nurse with the prince's cradle. It's... like a small bed."

"Is he in there?" I crane my neck but can't see inside it. The people are leaving the tables, moving toward the open floor. I shuffle forward with Kay, wondering how everyone knows what to do. They form a massive ring around the cradle but stop a good thirty feet away from it. How does this help us? I still can't see anything!

Now the king and queen appear, walking to the cradle. Lunilla's arm is curled around a small object wrapped in blankets and in the crook of her elbow I see the tiniest of faces.... *The baby!* My heart flies to the ceiling. I want to see it! I want to touch it!

The queen frustrates me enormously by lowering that perfect tiny face into the cradle. She stands with the king, the two beaming with pride. "Thank you all for coming to the celebration of our son, little Jack. He'll be your next king, you know!" She gives a smug smile. "At this time, we invite the fairies to bestow their gifts upon the prince.

May he grow into the best king this land has ever known and help us ensure that nothing evil ever returns to our kingdom."

The fairies drift out from the crowd, one by one. They are heavenly, like they're made of spring air and starlight. Their long hair floats, their dresses glow. Their feet are bare except for tiny flowers entwined around their toes.

And their gifts for the prince aren't booties and bells. Oh gobs, no. The first fairy waves her wand above the cradle and says, "Kindness." The next fairy waves her wand and says, "Courage." And it goes on from there, with the little prince receiving gifts of Health, Beauty, Charm, Passion, Strength, Happiness, Gentleness, Diligence and Confidence.

"Ugh." Kay gives a grimace. "When he grows up, he'll be so disgustingly perfect, everyone will hate him."

I lift an eyebrow. "What's wrong, didn't you get fairy gifts when you were born?"

"No." Kay scowls. "I was born in a prison."

"What?" I ask, wide-eyed. But we don't get time for an answer.

BANG! The double doors at the top of the stairs slam shut. A gust of wind rushes down through the ballroom, snuffing every candle and chandelier at once. The people gasp as our golden room drops into somber gray. I begin to smell smoke, just faintly, from the smothered wicks.

"What's happening?" I ask Kay.

"I don't know."

Smoke rises in thin gray lines from the candles on the tables, from the brackets on the walls, from the chandeliers above our heads. It should dissolve within seconds but it doesn't. If anything, it's getting thicker.

"Is there a fire?" someone cries. No, we can see there isn't. The room darkens as the windows get obscured by smoke. The shapes of the people become hazy. The snuffed wicks continue to pour smoke into the room; it sinks down from the ceiling, rises up from the floor.

I look down and can't see my feet. My eyes sting, my nostrils burn with the sharp stench of smoke. I'm coughing, coughing hard, and so is everyone else. But through that toxic fog we all hear a voice.

"And why wasn't I invited to the feast?"

Chapter 20

I try to squint through my watery eyes. But it's all gray fuzz. I hear a snap and see a momentary flare of light. The smoke begins to slide away from us. As quickly as it came, the smoke is drawn forward, gathering like a cloud near the front of the room. Then it swirls down, funneling into a point, and dissolves into the bowl of an old clay pipe. The pipe is held by a fairy.

Everyone stares, silent and shocked. Especially me. The wings tell me she's a fairy but she's not the pretty kind. She wears a faded green dress in bad need of ironing. Her gray hair looks like a lopsided mushroom planted on top of her head. She stands just a few steps up on the staircase and sucks the pipe from the corner of her mouth.

"Hmph. Cozy little gathering you've got here. Where's the brat?" She drops down the last few steps and the people split away from her, opening the way into the room. She sees the king and queen standing over the cradle. "Ooh, there he is! The little goosie."

"You're not WELCOME here!" Lunilla screams. She's bent over the cradle with her hand inside it and I imagine she was covering the baby's face when the smoke was on us.

"Well, *that* part I figured out when my invitation didn't show up." The old fairy struts forward, a hand on her hip. "And why not? I would've brought a nice gift for the little bambino."

"I don't want your gifts!" Lunilla hisses. "I don't want you anywhere near my child. Now GET OUT!"

"Or what, dearie? You'll do what?" The old fairy pokes the pipe in her mouth and waits for an answer. Curls of smoke leak out around her face.

The king holds up a hand. "Look – we didn't think you'd want to come anyway. We didn't think you'd take offense."

"That you wanted the other fairies and not me? Oh no, nothing personal there!"

"Of course, it's personal!" Lunilla cries. "You were the one who helped – HER! You *helped* her become the queen! While Melodie and I spent eight years in prison!"

"Hmm…. After which you escaped during the war, charmed the big fellow here, and the two of you took over the kingdom. So, I'd say you have little to complain about."

"You are Cinderella's fairy godmother," Lunilla says. "You will *never* be welcomed in my family!"

Oh my blood and bones. This is the wicked fairy. Who tried to kill Snowy but ended up killing my mother instead. The one known as Godnutter.

The old fairy – Godnutter – cocks her head. "So that's your answer? You won't ask me to stay?"

The king looks like he's considering it but Lunilla shouts, "Never!" And a hard silence falls, a silence that suddenly feels like a decision.

"As you wish." Godnutter smiles. "But I won't leave without first bestowing my gift on the prince. I've cooked up something special for him."

One of the young, pretty fairies lifts her hands. "Helena! The queen has asked you to go. Respect her wishes and leave this family in peace. You have done enough harm."

"Oh, I have not even begun!" Godnutter says. "You think I'll allow this, Lunilla? It's bad enough that you're on the throne the rightfully belongs to my Cindy. But now you plan to pass it on to your child! Mark my words, Cinderella will return, and every one of you will suffer for your treachery."

I frown. She must be mad. Not even magic can bring back the dead.

With a flick of her wings, Godnutter rises and hovers above the cradle. "Listen all!" She spreads her arms. "Your little prince shall grow in charm and courage and those other ridiculous things. I'll let you enjoy him for a little while. But he'll never have the throne that belongs to my goddaughter. On his sixteenth birthday – the year he comes of age - he shall prick his finger on the spindle of a spinning wheel... and drop dead!"

She aims the tip of her pipe at the cradle. A jet of white sparkles shoots out. But they don't strike the prince. At the last moment, a young girl springs out of the crowd and throws herself over the cradle.

Chapter 21

The sparkles strike the young woman, burst, and rain down on her body, dissolving into her hair and clothes. She straightens herself and faces the fairy. Kay draws a sharp breath.

Godnutter looks shocked. "BEAUTY!" Her voice snaps across the air like ice cracking. "Stupid girl! What have you done!"

"You can't just curse a baby!" the girl shouts.

"You just cursed yourself!" Godnutter says. "It's on *you* now!"

"So? Just take it off me! It's your curse."

"Because it's my curse, I *can't* take it off you!" Godnutter says. "You should know that!"

"You told me all magic can be reversed!"

"Not like that!" Godnutter snaps her fingers. "What were you thinking! Why didn't you stay at home?"

"I wasn't missing the party just because *you* weren't invited. I have my own life!"

Godnutter stares at her and slowly shakes her head. "Not for much longer, you don't. You'll be sixteen next month."

Wow. Rotten luck. So, *this* is Beauty. I study her with curiosity. It's hard for me to tell what people consider beautiful but she's pleasant to look at. Her eyes have lots of lashes around them and her cheeks are a pretty color. She has dark brown hair that drops around her in long, wavy lines. And her dress is gold. And by that, I don't mean burnt ochre or bright yellow, I mean *gold*. Like someone melted it and wove it into a dress.

Lunilla is looking quite pleased with all this. She scoops the baby out of the cradle and rubs his back. "Well! I guess your curse was a total flop. Not the first time that's happened to you, is it? Maybe you should find a new hobby."

Godnutter swings her arm around to point the pipe at Lunilla. She flinches back, turning her shoulder to shield the baby. Beauty leaps out to grab Godnutter's arm but Cooper swoops in and grabs Beauty. He lifts her off the ground, one arm around her waist, and with his free hand, yanks a dagger from his belt. He pokes the tip of it against her neck. "Get out of here now, witch," he growls at Godnutter. "Or your daughter won't live another sixteen seconds, let alone years."

There's a murmur of alarm among the people, a flutter of disturbance from the fairies. One of them drifts outward and to my surprise, it's a man. As in, a male fairy. "Pardon me," he says. "I have not yet bestowed my gift upon the prince."

"What's THAT got to do with anything?" Beauty shrieks, still pinned against Cooper. The fairy man smiles like there's nothing odd in this. I like his eyes, brown and soft as a deer's. He looks kind. "My gift for the prince was to be protection from harm. But I think Beauty might benefit more from it."

"No, she won't!" Godnutter shouts. "Your magic is too young, Hunter. It won't work!"

Did she say Hunter? Did she say *Hunter?* Oh, you have GOT to be kidding me! That's *him?* Oh my blood and bones - that's him. He fits every detail Snowy ever told me about him. The dark hair and eyes, the gentle expression, the lean and muscular body. His clothes are different than she described, he wears a wrap-around tunic, tied with a cord, loose pants, and light sandals. Snowy never said he was a fairy. She said he died!

Hunter (I still don't believe it) lifts a hand. "You're quite right. I'm not saying the curse can be lifted. But I think it can be lessened. Instead of dying, Beauty will fall into a deep sleep. It may last a very long time. But she will have the possibility of being awakened." He looks at the king. "Let her go, Cooper."

I don't expect the king to comply but he does. Just nods and puts her down. Hunter makes a soft gesture with his wand and a spray of gold sparkles falls over

Beauty. She stands still while they settle. "I don't feel any different."

Hunter smiles and I instantly forgive Snowy for all her moping and mooning. He is beautiful. "You'll be fine, Beauty. Don't worry."

"Oh, that's fine to you?" Godnutter cries. "Everyone in my family under a curse, sentenced to sleep in a box? Oh yes, very fine indeed!" She grabs Beauty's arm and with the pipe shoots a jet of smoke at the ground. It sprays upward and with a harsh *BANG!* the two of them disappear.

Chapter 22

The smoke dissolves. A hush follows. Not exactly silence, more like rustles and whimpers. The people look at each other and then at the queen.

She's still clasping the baby against her. But she lets out a sigh that's almost a laugh. "There, there, my friends. Let us all catch our breath. The wicked fairy did not succeed, she tried to curse my child and instead she cursed her own. Sometimes the world IS fair." She grins and a few people chuckle nervously.

"But what about Beauty!" Kay cries. "She doesn't deserve this! Though the curse was lessened, she'll still be lost to us!"

"Not our problem," Lunilla says.

"We have to help her," Kay says.

Lunilla shrugs and shifts her gaze to me. "Oh! Almost forgot about you in this mess." She hands the baby over to the king and beckons to me with her finger. "Come with me, Runzel."

I look at Kay. He shrugs, annoyed, and I suspect his thoughts are far away from me. He's worried about *her*. I shake my head and walk away from him.

Lunilla marches ahead of me through the ballroom without turning to see if I follow her. I don't like her any better from the back, her red squiggles of hair bouncing, her skirt swelling out like a purple hill. She takes me back to where the tables are, through an archway in the wall. We pass through a narrow corridor heavy with the smell of grease and I wonder if the kitchen is nearby.

We turn into another long corridor. Two young girls in aprons scurry out of our way like mice into cracks in the wall. Lunilla stops at a plain wooden door about halfway down.

"Faster this way," she says. "We're going to the garden."

"Oh."

She opens the door and cool air flows into my face. With it comes a mixture of wonderful smells, almost entirely new to me. I step out onto a tidy dirt path and instead of lifeless snow, there is green all around me. Bushes that grow in leafy walls along the paths which are straight as ribbons and cross at the center of the garden. Plants laid out in beds of perfect circles with low stone walls around them. Pale statues of ladies that rise out of the greenery and wear loose dresses that seem to be falling off of them. But what grips me the most are the clusters of color I see growing on the bushes.

I draw my breath. "Are those the roses?"

"Pretty, aren't they?" Lunilla nudges up a heavy blossom with her finger. "They're enchanted. Know what that means?"

"It means they're magic." Gently, I reach out and touch the rose nearest to me. It feels soft and loving, like a kiss. The petals swirl around each other and curl out at the edges. It's even more beautiful than a frozen spider web.

Lunilla strolls down the path, stopping here and there to pluck dead leaves off the bushes. "Each one has a different magical quality," she says. "The red roses are for beauty. The pink roses make you feel happy when you smell them and they can also be used for love spells. The blue roses are calming, they relieve your anxieties, but if you consume too much, you'll forget everything you ever knew."

"Goodness." I shy away from the nearest bush that holds a bunch of blue roses. They do have a mysterious beauty about them, like each one is holding a secret.

We're nearing the corning of the garden and fall into the shadow of the castle wall which looms over us on two sides. The bushes here must get very little sunlight and yet....

"Oh my blood and bones," I say.

Lunilla grins. "These are my favorite. The black roses. Aren't they gorgeous?"

They're scary. Black roses, black as dirt, blooming in this dim corner of the garden. Their stems and leaves are a dry sort of gray, like all the color was leached out of them. And yet they don't appear to be dying.

"What do these do?" I ask.

"Oh, these have a lot of... interesting uses. But you have to be careful. Every part of the plant is dangerous."

"I'm not surprised." I turn my head. I can't look at the black roses anymore. I retreat up the path, back into the sun, and stop beside the pink roses. I feel like crying for no apparent reason.

Lunilla strolls up behind me. "All right, Runzel?"

"I'm tired." I drop my arms and let my braid slide off to the ground. I can't carry it anymore, it's too heavy.

Lunilla folds her arms and stares at it. "Only the daughter of Cinderella would wear a hairpiece that long. She was always desperate for attention too, had a sickening obsession with her looks. Do you know who I am?"

"You're the queen."

"Yes, of course, that's not what I meant. I mean I used to know your mother."

"Oh! Were you her friend?"

The queen laughs and it sounds like honking. "Not a chance! She was my stepsister. We grew up together in the same house."

"What's a stepsister?"

"Oh gracious, I'm not explaining all that. We lived as sisters but we weren't, that's all you need to know. We let Cindy live with us when her pa passed away."

"So – so you knew her when she was a girl?"

"Oh yes."

"What was she like?"

"Ugly," Lunilla says. "And snooty too. Always thought herself better than the rest of us. A sneak and a liar and a tramp. That was Cinderella."

Her words hit me like slaps on blistered skin. I hoped, I really hoped, that Snowy was wrong about my mother. But this person is saying she was bad, too. I feel like curling up and crying. I feel ashamed.

Lunilla enjoys my pain, I can see it. She tilts her head as she looks at me. "You're a lot like her. The dark streak is there, you just haven't unleashed it. Where's the other one?"

"The other what?" I mumble.

"The other twin. Cinderella had twins, Cooper told me. Where is she?"

"I don't know. She was stolen by-" I gasp. She was stolen by a wicked fairy. I have known this all my life. And yet, when the wicked fairy was right in front of me, I failed to put it together. Until now.

Beauty!

No way. No *way*. We look nothing alike! But the story fits, all of it. Her age, her brown hair, her fairy godmother. Beauty, the girl that Kay loves. She is my sister.

"What's wrong?" Lunilla asks.

I pat my chest. "Sorry, I... I had a pain. Uh, my twin was stolen by a plague. It's just me now."

Lunilla smirks. "You're lying. But I expect that from Cinderella's daughter. Don't you trust me?"

"Not at all." I don't care if she gets mad. I need to talk to Beauty. I can't say this is *good* news – I feel distinctly let down - but a long-time question has been answered. She deserves to know. And the queen does not.

Lunilla sidles over and pats my shoulder. "Come on, Runzel, I won't hurt you. I just want to know some stuff. No harm in that."

I twist away from her and meet her eyes. "Fine. I'll trade you. A question for a question."

Lunilla narrows her eyes. "Fine. But I go first."

"It was my idea. How did you get these flowers?"

Lunilla shrugs. "The palace has always had a rose garden. They didn't used to be magic, though. But when the kingdom froze over, the roses did not. They drew from the magic in the earth to stay alive. Cooper thinks they might've been blessed by a fairy long ago. We're not really sure."

"The black roses too?"

"It's my turn to ask," she says. "Where do you live? Why have I never seen you before?"

"That's two questions." I glare at her. "But I guess they both have the same answer. Like you, I've been kept inside a tower. *For my entire life.* That's why you've never seen me."

Lunilla looks at my braid on the ground and draws a noisy breath. "That's not a piece, is it? It's your real hair."

Her eyes bulge. "You're the girl who lives with the Ice Witch! Aren't you?"

"It's my turn to ask!"

"NO!" She grabs my arm with a savage face. "Kay told me about you: a girl with long hair kept in a tower by the Ice Witch. He said he was going to get her out. That's YOU, isn't it?"

"Let go of me!" I try to yank myself away but her grip is surprisingly strong. She smiles, baring all of her long teeth. "Well done, Kay! He just delivered BOTH of my enemies bottled up in one scrawny girl." She jerks my body against hers, facing outward. I try to struggle. Almost too easily, she jerks me along the path, back to where the black rose bushes are. Crouching over me, she forces me down and shoves my face into a fat blossom.

"Smell THAT, Cindy's daughter," she growls.

I can't help it. I'm panting and the odor fills my head. It smells sharp and angry, like skunk. It smells like hate. It smells like fear.

It smells like death.

Chapter 23

I wake up. It's very dark. I blink heavy eyelids, don't understand and don't try. I'm so tired. The darkness is comforting.

Smell returns to me first. Cold stones. Damp earth. Dead animal, faintly. Human waste, more strongly. I start to wonder but I'm still so tired.

As wakefulness returns, I take in more. I'm in a small, stone room with a dirt floor. There are no windows, no furniture, and no people. Just a door made of metal bars and beyond that, a dark space.

I stand slowly, walking my hands up the wall. My braid is all over the floor. A reddish light burns outside the metal door, like a torch lit close to my room. I walk to the door. There's a narrow corridor on my right and left, and straight across from me, another door made of bars. No one is there.

"Snowy?" I call out – and flinch back. My voice sounds enormous. "Snowy? Where am I?"

"She's not here," a new voice says. I gasp and jerk my head to the brighter end of the corridor. A woman slides into view and stops in front of me. I don't know her at all.

"What do you want?" I ask. She frightens me. Her face is pale. Her hair is limp. And her eyes have no light in them. She wears a thin dress of grayish blue with no decorations.

The lady looks at me with no expression. "I just wanted to see if you look like Cinderella." She has a bored, colorless way of speaking. "You do. You look like her before she made the changes to herself. The old Cinderella."

"Who are you?"

"Melodie. The queen's sister. I heard about you from my son."

"Are you... Kay's mother?"

Melodie nods. "He seems to like you a lot. He's a good boy."

"Where is he?"

"Asleep. We told him the queen sent you home in a private carriage – you were sick. He was very upset and wanted to go after you. But we told him to wait for tomorrow. You've been unconscious a long time, it's nearly midnight.

"What!" I grab the bars of my door. "I have to go home! Snowy doesn't know where I am!"

"Neither do you, do you?" Melodie says. "You're in a dungeon below the palace. And you're staying. You're the queen's prisoner now."

"Why?"

"She wants to use you to flush out the Ice Witch. You're the bait. She'll have to come here and do what we say."

I almost laugh. "You can't control Snowy! She will freeze you, *all* of you, the second she gets here. You won't even touch her!"

Melodie shrugs. "We'll see." She bends over and coughs into her sleeve. The cough sounds terrible – harsh and wet.

"What's wrong?"

Melodie sighs. "I'm sick. The tower we were kept in... it was never warm enough. A sickness got into my chest and it's never left. Some days I can barely breathe."

"Didn't they give you medicine?"

"In prison, no one cares if you die. Except for one guard, for a little while. He took me out for air and let me walk by the sea – our prison was along the coast. I was happy with him. But it didn't last."

"Why not?"

Melodie shrugs. "We grew tired of each other. It happens. But he gave me Kay, so it was worth it."

"Oh," I say, not really understanding. I don't think Kay looks much like her. And this woman seems so tired and dull, like she has no happy feelings inside. She reminds me of Snowy.

"Did you know my mother?" I ask.

Melodie nods.

"Could you... tell me something about her? Something good?"

Melodie's dead expression stays dead. "Hard to say. She killed *my* mother and threw me and my sister in prison. So, I'm not the best one to ask."

My heart sinks. "You didn't like her, either?"

"She did it to herself. She could've had friends but she chose to be cruel. If she returned, you'd hate her, too."

"No, I wouldn't!" I say. But Melodie is leaving. She takes the torch with her and ignores me when I cry out. I'm left alone in the dark and in the blindness. This is worse than my tower. I cover my mouth and shiver through a few quiet sobs. I hate not seeing. And even though she's dead and gone, I'm feeling sorry for my mother. I didn't want it to be true but I guess it is: nobody loved her.

Chapter 24

I don't sleep. I can't possibly lie down on a floor of
bare dirt. I pace across the hours, endless and black,
my head squirming with questions. Those hours of total
darkness are the worst things I've ever experienced. I
can't handle no light, no sight.

My legs ache. I try to crouch against the metal door
and lean my head on the bars. I guess I doze off for a
while because my eyes jump open when I hear someone
screaming. I stand up. Light is moving up the corridor;
I hear footsteps and voices. Someone is screaming and
crying at once.

Two men with thick arms and frowning faces come
into view. They hold a girl between them, gripping her
arms and partly dragging her. The girl is Beauty.

"I'm not! I'm NOT! Please, let me go, the queen is
insane! Please, you must listen! It's not ME!" Her face is
soaking in tears.

The two men don't speak at all. They open the door
opposite mine, shove Beauty in, and bang it shut. She's

still pleading and crying. The men leave but – thankfully
- drop their torch into a bracket by her cell. At least we
can see.

I stand at my door, watching Beauty cry. But an odd
thing happens. Once the men are out of sight, she immediately stops. She wipes her cheeks with both hands
and flicks away the tears. "Well, that didn't work."

"What didn't?" I ask.

She looks startled and stares across the hall at me.
"Who are you?"

"Rapunzel."

Her fancy eyes slide over me, up and down. I stare at
her, too. She's not wearing the gold dress anymore. This
one is more simple, reddish in color, with a belt of dark
brown, like her hair. The kind of dress you'd wear every
day. Other than her looking my age and my height, I see
nothing to mark us as sisters.

She turns her eyes away. "You were at the party last
night. I saw your hair."

"Yes."

"With Prince Kay, were you not?" she asks.

I nod but I don't want to talk to her about Kay. "Why
are you here?" I ask.

"Ugh!" Beauty shakes her head. "The queen has lost
it. She asked to see me this morning and oh – silly me! I
thought she would thank me for *saving her child*. But no,
not a word about it! She just asked me a lot of strange
questions about my childhood and then out *nowhere*,

114

she yells, 'YOU ARE CINDERELLA'S DAUGHTER!' It's lunacy!"

"Why is it lunacy?"

"Because I'm not!" Beauty cries. "My mother died when I was a baby, I live with my fairy godmother. I'm not the daughter of the friggin' Cursed Queen!"

I frown, confused. Then I realize something. Beauty doesn't know the truth. And I do. I know something she doesn't. It feels so good, for once, to not be the ignorant one.

"You *are* Cinderella's daughter," I say.

"I'm not!"

"Yes, you are. That's why you're here. That's why I'm here, too. Both of us are Cinderella's daughters." I don't make a big thing of it. She probably won't like it that we're sisters – I don't. But she should know.

Beauty goes very quiet. So I tell her about Snowy and Cinderella and the twins. About the one who was stolen by a wicked fairy and never found. Beauty doesn't move as she listens to my story. She barely blinks.

"Godnutter was... always vague about my mother," Beauty says softly. "When I was younger, I once asked her what my mother's name was. She said Agatha. The next day, I wanted to write it down and asked her how to spell it – and she spelled it as Agnes. When I asked, she laughed at me and said I made a mistake. But I knew I hadn't. She was making it all up."

Beauty looks at me, really looks this time. "You look nothing like me."

I shrug. "So what?"

Beauty taps her lip with her finger. "So Lunilla isn't the true queen." Her eyes widen. "It should be me!"

"No, it should be me," I say.

Beauty narrows her eyes. She strokes back her hair, sliding her fingers around her face. "If you've spent your whole life inside a tower, you wouldn't know the first thing about ruling a kingdom. Besides, I was born first."

"We were born at the same time."

Beauty laughs. "There, you see? You know nothing! Even if we're twins, one of us was born first. And I'm clearly more mature than you." Her long lashes flick over me. "Your body isn't even womanly yet."

I flinch and cover my chest with my hand. I'm a little womanly, just not as much as her. Her body is all wavy and mine is straight. Still... my hair is a lot longer.

Beauty shakes her head. "And to think, I've been to see the Cursed Queen three times."

"The Cursed Queen?"

"Yeah, have you seen her?"

"I did today. Who is she?"

"You don't know?" Beauty puts her face to bars, eyes alive with excitement. "That's her! That's Cinderella!"

I step back from the door. "What?"

Beauty nods emphatically.

"But... Snowy said she was dead," I whisper.

116

"Snowy lied," Beauty says.

I hold my elbows and turn aside. The lady in the box – the Cursed Queen – Cinderella - my *mother.* That was her, with the golden hair and little heart-shaped mouth. Asleep in a box – but not dead.

"Can we wake her up?" I ask.

"No," Beauty says. "Godnutter told me about it. She needs to be kissed and it has to be true love." Beauty rolls her eyes. "Not likely to happen at this point."

"No. No one ever loved her," I mumble.

"Except Hunter," Beauty says.

I look up slowly. "Uh, what?"

"Hunter. The fairy who tried to lessen my curse? He was in love with Snow White but then he fell for Cinderella. He was going to kiss her and wake her up. But Snow White was so jealous, she killed him so that Cinderella couldn't have him."

Is... that... so! This is one story Snowy didn't tell me! She always said his death was an accident and she *never* said he left her for Cinderella! No wonder she tried so hard to convince me that no one loved my mother. And why she got so angry about it.

But I feel strange, now. Like I thought I was walking on solid earth and now it cracks and slides. Snowy has been lying to me. Lying for years. She told me my mother was dead, said it over and over without blinking. But all this time, my mother was asleep in a box. Snowy must have known, yet she never took me to see her.

She just locked me away and didn't care.

Chapter 25

That evening – at least, I think it's evening – Melodie comes back. She brings us mats of thick wool, rolled up and tied. "You shouldn't have to sleep on the floor," she says.

"When do we get food?" I ask. I've been hungry for hours and my lips are sticking together. There's nothing in here, not even a pail of water to sip from.

"Soon." Melodie squeezes the rolled mat between the bars of my door. It smells dusty. She steps across the hall and gives the other one to Beauty.

"Oh sure, like I'd really sleep on that." Beauty grabs the mat and throws it into a corner of her cell. "Could you please explain why you're treating us like criminals just because we're the daughters of Cinderella?"

"Oh, now you believe it?" Melodie says.

Beauty points at me with her chin. "That one explained it to me."

"She has a name," Melodie says.

"I forgot it. So, how long are we here for?"

"I don't know," Melodie says. "Until Lunilla lets you out, I guess."

Beauty holds up one of her pale, pointy fingers. "I am *not* staying here in this rat hole. If you don't release me, Godnutter will. And she won't be too happy with you."

Melodie smirks. "I'm afraid 'that one' tried a similar threat. But so far, neither the Ice Witch nor the Wicked Fairy has arrived to save you. So, you might need the mat." She heads up the hall, silent except for the soft echo of her coughs.

Beauty stands at the door, arms folded, foot tapping. "Godnutter better get here soon. If this is some 'lesson' she's trying to teach me...."

"I know. I hope Snow will come too," I say.

"She always yelled at me for not listening. This is probably her way of punishing me for going to the party." She rolls her eyes and blinks twice, like Kay said she did. "She makes too many rules."

"So, you live with her?" I ask.

Beauty nods. "Not as much as I used to. I often skip out and stay with my friends. Our home is a four-day journey from here – a little village by the sea. Honestly, it's so dead. We have some sheep and she taught me to spin wool. Wanted me to grow into 'a good, wholesome girl.'"

I get the feeling that didn't work.

"She was nuts," Beauty says. "Always told me I was pretty but got mad if someone else did. Didn't allow me to learn dancing because it might attract the boys. I couldn't have a red dress because she thinks that color is *naughty*. And using magic was completely forbidden."

I find all of this strangely comforting. Beauty has problems. Her life isn't perfect. Like me, she lives with someone who makes her feel trapped. I feel so much better now.

"Snowy makes a lot of rules too," I say.

"I have my own life! I don't have to listen to her, she's not my mother. Nobody likes her, anyway. I mean, she dresses like a beggar, she smokes like a furnace, it was embarrassing just to be seen with her."

I frown. So far, Beauty has barely acknowledged a single thing I said. She doesn't care about my problems but expects me to listen to hers. It seems very rude.

I raise my voice. "Aren't you worried about the curse?" I say, cutting off whatever rubbish she's going on about now. She blinks at me, disoriented.

"Nope!" Beauty smiles and strokes her hair again. "Godnutter will figure it out. She's one of the most powerful fairies in the land."

"Did she tell you that herself?"

"And there's plenty of time. I won't be sixteen until the end of next month."

I stare at her. "When?"

"The last day of October. Don't you even know the day we were born?"

Yes, I do. And it's not the end of October. That's very weird. If we're twins, we were born on the same day... right? But her day is way off. There has to be a mistake but I can't figure it out. Maybe I should mention this to her.

Or... maybe not.

I mean, it's not like she would *listen* to me.

Chapter 26

A servant brings us each a bowl of stew. I'm so hungry, it tastes like the best stuff on earth. It's got beef in it, which I rarely get at home. But Beauty complains. It's not warm enough, the beef is old, the carrots are mushy. We deserve so much better, blah, blah, blah.

Over the next two hours, she goes completely nuts! Starts pacing around her cell, making angry little squeaks. Mutters things like "ridiculous" and "unbelievable" and makes random threats to break out on her own. I guess I'm more used to small spaces than she is.

"I'm so BORED!" she screams at the ceiling.

"Will you SHUT UP!" I say. "You're making it worse!"

"This is *your* fault!" Beauty says. "You had to come blazing into the palace, announcing to the *whole world* that you were Cinderella's daughter. I heard you! And now we're stuck here because you made the queen feel threatened."

We hear a nasal laugh in the corridor and the swish of a heavy skirt. Beauty rolls her eyes. "Oh, here we go."

"So, that's what you think? That I'm scared of you?" Lunilla saunters into view between our two cells. She's stuffed inside a bulbous, bright-orange dress, bursting with pink lace trimmings, and just looks like a giant mistake. "I have you both right where I want you. So, what's to feel threatened about?"

"Where's Godnutter?" Beauty asks. "Why hasn't she come for me?"

"Haven't seen her since the party," Lunilla says. "But if you think about it, there's really no point in her saving you. You're going to drop dead, anyway. So, why should she waste her time?"

"I am *not* dropping dead!" Beauty says.

"What about Snowy?" I ask.

Lunilla turns her curly head to look at me. She smells like the rose garden but also like some kind of sour, fruity drink. "Not yet. I had a message sent to your little tower home. If she's smart, she'll come here soon."

"Why do you want her?"

Lunilla smirks and doesn't answer. With great ease, she strolls between our cells, emphasizing each shift from heel to toe. "Can't believe you girls are finally here. I've been looking for you for years and years, ever since the day I became queen."

"Really?" Beauty says.

"Cooper told me all about it. Cinderella had two little girlies, of course she would. And then got herself poisoned! Best news I ever had in my life. Snow White ran away with the babies and that's all anyone knew. Cooper thought they probably died without their mother but I didn't. And I couldn't risk them growing up and coming back to steal my throne." She pauses. "Which one of you is older?"

"I am," Beauty and I say together.

Lunilla laughs. "It really doesn't matter now. So - I had my spies search for Snow White. But they couldn't find her. And a few of them never came back – I think *she* found them first." Lunilla glowers. "So then I had to employ... harsher methods."

"What does that mean?" Beauty asks.

I clench my fists. "It means the Beast."

"Ooh! You're a smartie," Lunilla says.

Beauty, who had been clasping the bars of her door, drops her hands and steps back. "You have the Beast?"

Lunilla smiles.

"Kay told me you didn't!" I shout. "He said you had nothing to do with it!"

"Kay's such a sweet boy," Lunilla says. "I didn't want to upset him. He doesn't know what it takes to rule a kingdom, sometimes."

"Where is it?" Beauty asks in a breathless voice. "Where do you keep it?"

"Oh, like I would tell you that!" Lunilla says. "Believe me, if you find out, it won't be a very good day. Anyway, I was getting so frustrated. And then Cooper said to me, 'How do we know Snow White is still raising those girls?

125

She could have dumped them in an orphanage or given them to a new family.' Snow White – so I've heard – was a selfish little brat and we didn't think motherhood would suit her for long."

I sigh. I wish it hadn't.

"So, it could be any girl, I thought. Any girl in the kingdom. All I knew for certain was the age. But I was smart about it. It would be wasteful to kill off every fifteen-year-old girl indiscriminately. I'm not like that, I'm not a bad person."

Oh my blood and bones.

"So, I gathered my spies again and I said, 'Find me orphans. Any girl of about fifteen who does not seem to be living with her parents.' She smiles at Beauty. "You were on the list, my dear."

Beauty gasps.

Lunilla gives her honking laugh. "I didn't think it was you! I thought Cindy's daughters would be blonde, like her. Cooper couldn't remember, you know how *men* are. So I started with blondes. I asked my spies to bring me a handkerchief, a stocking, anything with the girl's scent on it. And then I gave it to the Beast before I let him out at night. It's been very effective!"

Beauty staggers away from her door. I clench the bars and bare my teeth. "You're a horrible person. When Snowy comes, I'll tell her to freeze your eyeballs first!"

"Snow White won't be able to touch me so long as I have you," Lunilla says. "You were so adorable! Walking right up to me at the party and telling me who you were. Like a birthday gift! The only problem was you didn't know your twin. All you said was, 'she was stolen.' And then I remembered: the fairies told me that Cinderella's godmother was in disgrace because she had stolen a baby. I called for Beauty and asked her what she knew about her mother. She didn't know much but had been told that her mother had freakishly small feet." Lunilla smiles. "That did it for me."

"All right, we're here! Now what?" Beauty asks.

Lunilla folds her arms. "I'm waiting for Snow White. She needs to get rid of this wretched eternal winter. It's no fun ruling a kingdom that's always cold and miserable. Enough is enough! I won't let her see Runzel until she does it."

I snort. Good luck with that.

Lunilla's face hardens. "But once she does, I won't need her anymore. Or the two of you, either. All that's left of Cinderella's filth must be purged. So, enjoy your short time together as sisters. Because once this is over, I'm feeding you to the Beast."

Chapter 27

It's a hard night. I resist as long as I can and then collapse on the mat from pure exhaustion. It's actually a blessing - Beauty's crying was driving me nuts! And I don't think she was faking this time. I understand – I'm pretty scared too – but I still have faith in Snowy. She will come and crush them all.

I dream about it. Snowy comes to the palace. She stands before it in her white fur coat and lifts her arms to the sky. Ice begins to grow over the castle, pale blue and sparkling. It covers everything - the walls, the gardens, the people. Servants turn to ice statues in the middle of their tasks. I have a distinct image of Lunilla in her throne, frozen with her mouth wide open. Then Snowy and I hook elbows and leave the palace, laughing.

But I wake up and Snowy hasn't come. I wait for her through a long and dreary day. Beauty and I don't speak. I sit on the mat, unbraid my hair, comb it with my fingers, and braid it up again. Takes me three hours.

It's gotten very dirty from the floor and I pick out bits of leaves and even a few bugs. I really need Snowy to come and wash it.

I don't like it here. I want to go back to my tower, at least there I had a window. My eyes are tired of this feeble torch light and my stomach grumbles for food. Nobody comes to see us until evening, when Melodie brings us bowls of broth and dry bread. I sit cross-legged on the mat, dunking each chunk of bread into the broth. It's not enough. I curl myself up on the mat and hug my braid with my knees. I fall asleep thinking about Kay.

I don't know if it's morning when I wake up. But it feels like I've slept all night. I rub my face, get up and hobble to the door, kicking my braid out of the way. Beauty is standing at her own door. She puts a finger to her lips and widens her eyes.

"What's wrong?" I say.

"Shh!" Beauty says. "I heard something!"

I listen but don't hear a thing. I press my face to the bars and try to peer down the corridor. She's focused on the opposite direction from which our visitors normally come.

"What did it sound like?" I ask.

"Like stones scraping... and something moving. It sounded big."

My scalp crinkles. She can't be serious. "Maybe it's just a rat. They get into my tower, sometimes. They can sound really big when they move around."

"Shut UP!" Beauty snaps. "I'm trying to listen!" Her piercing blue eyes are on me at the moment. But when she turns them back to the corridor, she shrieks.

I jerk back. A short figure has appeared between our two cells, covered in a black cloak and hood. Two pasty-white hands emerge from the cloak. The figure reaches up and pushes back the hood. I gasp.

"Snowy!" I rush to the door. I was never so glad to see her cold, white face. With that black cloak on, she looks paler than usual, almost ghostly. She fires a look at me and presses a finger to her lips.

I drop my voice to a whisper. "Snowy, where did you come from?"

Snowy points to the corridor behind her. "I know a secret way in. There's an old well out in The Wood that has a tunnel into the castle. I don't think anyone knows about it but me. It leads into this dungeon." She gives Beauty a curious glance.

"Why'd you sneak in?" I ask. "I thought you'd come blasting in here!"

Snowy shakes her head. "Too much trouble. We can sneak out and just disappear. I guess we'll have to find a new place to live, the queen knows about our tower." She gives me a withering look. "You've been lying to me, Rapunzel."

"Well, *you* lied to me! I've learned a lot since I left, you've been lying to me for years. Oh, and guess who *that* is." I point across the hall at Beauty, who has been quietly staring at Snowy.

"Who?" Snowy asks. I give her a pointed look. Snowy looks at Beauty for a long moment and her eyes widen. "Oh my stars, it can't be."

"That's why we're locked up," I say. "The queen knows who we are."

Snowy steps closer to the door and stares at Beauty, who returns the gaze without shyness. Snowy presses a hand to her chest. "Look at you. Look at those eyes. It's like seeing my father again."

"Really?" Beauty says, surprisingly soft. "I look like my father?"

"Very much," Snowy says. Now that they're standing near each other, I see they both have the same narrow nose. This is getting creepy.

"Are you the Ice Witch?" Beauty asks. Snowy nods. "And I'm your sister. So is Rapunzel."

"*Her* I met," Beauty says. "Not to rush things, but... could you get us out, please? The queen wants to feed us to the Beast."

Snowy sighs. "Amazing. Only one day out of her tower and Rapunzel gets herself thrown in prison and sentenced to death." She shoots me a hard look.

I fold my arms. "I met a Dwarf in The Wood, too."

"Then you're lucky he didn't kill you." Snowy studies the padlock on Beauty's door, touches the keyhole with her finger.

"And I saw my mother."

Snowy's eyelids falter for just a moment. She sets her jaw and cups her hand over the lock. I can't see what she's does but moments later, a thick shard of ice is sticking out of the keyhole. Snowy twists it to one side and the lock pops open.

She crosses to my door and picks up the padlock. When the lock springs open, she finally looks at me. "She's never coming back, Rapunzel. Now get your hair and let's go."

I grab a piece of my braid but let the rest of it drag. "You should've told me," I say. I march out of the cell to where Beauty is waiting.

"Is *she* coming with us?" I ask.

"I won't leave her behind," Snowy says. "We can take her as far as the well. Where do you live... girl?"

"My name is Beauty. And don't worry, once I'm out, I'll be fine."

"Do we have to do it this way?" I ask Snowy. "Aren't you angry they locked me up here? Don't you think the queen should be taught a lesson?" I'm sorry but I hate the idea of sneaking out like scared children. The Snow Queen is here and gob dash it, I want an ice storm.

"Yes, I am," Snowy says. "But they invited me here, which means they probably intend to threaten me in some way. That's why I snuck in, I'm not walking into a trap."

"They can't trap you!" I cry.

"Even magic has limitations," Snowy says. "I'm not going to push my luck."

I stomp my foot. "Why? Why do you have to be like that? Always sneaking and hiding from everyone. You're such a coward!"

Snowy grabs my arm. "Quiet! I don't have to explain myself to you! Now march yourself up this hallway or I'll...." She looks past me and her pale face goes paler. "Get behind me!" she hisses.

"Why?"

Snowy shoves me behind her and steps in front of me and Beauty. And then I see why: the king is here. I guess we didn't hear him coming during our fight. Snowy throws out her arms and spreads her fingers.

"Easy, easy...." Cooper holds up his large hand. "It's all right, Snowy. I thought I heard your voice."

"Stay away from us," Snowy says.

Cooper takes a casual step backward. "Just wanted to see you, that's all. Been a long time, hasn't it?"

Snowy keeps her hands raised. She doesn't take her eyes off Cooper.

"Did you know I was king?" he asks.

Snowy nods. "I've heard the name."

"You look the same as you used to," Cooper says. "Only more sad. Where've you been?"

"Not far. I found a place to hide. Where are your brothers?"

"Here and there. We've spread out a bit. Barker is still at the cottage."

"I see." Snowy doesn't relax her attack stance.

"Why'd you make it cold?" Cooper asks.

Snowy shrugs. "I was angry."

"Still?"

"Aren't you?"

Cooper surprises me by smiling. "Naw, not any more. It's good to see you, Snowy."

Snowy lowers her hands. A tiny smile pulls at her lips. "Thank you. I – I've missed you guys."

Cooper beckons with a jerk of his head. "Come on upstairs! Meet the wife."

"Oh, I don't...."

"Nothing to worry about. Look, as I recall, you didn't like Cinderella much. Neither did my wife, so you'll get along great. Come on upstairs and talk to her, we just want to warm up the kingdom, that's all. She's a great girl."

"She locked away my sisters," Snowy says.

"And said she's feeding us to the Beast!" Beauty cries.

Cooper waves a hand. "Aw, she gets like that when she's worked up, doesn't mean a word of it. You got nothing to worry about. Come on, Snowy, come up and have a mutton joint with us."

Snowy is smiling. There's a sparkle in her eyes I'm not used to seeing. I think she's happy to see her friend. She clears her throat and tries to assume a serious face. "Very well. I will grant her a short audience."

Beauty looks horrified but I'm ready to cheer. I know Lunilla by now. There's no way this is going to go well.

Chapter 28

Cooper takes us to a room I haven't seen before. It has a long, shiny floor with a strip of purple rug running over it. Lunilla sits at the end of the rug, in a big chair. She's speaking to a man who wears a greasy apron and I wonder if he works in the kitchen. When she sees us, she waves him off.

Lunilla stands as we approach. She doesn't seem to notice anyone but Snowy and her normally smug face is quite serious. She lifts a hand and we stop about ten feet from her chair.

Cooper clears his throat. "My dear, this is Snow White. She's come to talk peacefully."

"Why – why are the girls here too?" Lunilla asks.

"She let them out," Cooper says.

Lunilla looks at Snowy, who gives a nod. Carefully, Lunilla sinks back into her chair. I honestly think she's scared of Snowy and is trying not to show it.

Snowy clasps her hands behind her back. "It's been a long time since I've seen this room." She glances at a tapestry of bright flowers that hangs on the wall behind Lunilla. "Your taste is better than Cinderella's."

Lunilla's smirk begins to bloom. "Indeed. When I got here, most of the palace was dirt black. It needed some color."

"It needed anything that wasn't Cinderella," Snowy says. Her eyebrows shoot up. "Oh my stars, you're using that chair?"

I already noticed it. Lunilla's chair looks like a giant piece of glass. It's shiny and cut into flat sections, like a diamond, but I don't think it's a diamond. Just a big, transparent rock.

Lunilla smiles. "They told me it was Cinderella's and that's why I keep it. A reminder that I have her throne."

I clench my teeth. I don't like it that they're trashing my mother. Beauty looks annoyed, too.

"So. You're the Ice Witch?" Lunilla asks.

Snowy shrugs. "I suppose I am."

"Why do you make it snow all the time? Nobody likes it, you know. Don't you get tired of the cold?"

"It never bothered me," Snowy says. "And it kept us safe, made our home harder to find." She waves a hand at me and Beauty. "I came here to fetch my sister and the girl who is her twin. All I ask is that you let us leave. You have nothing to fear from me."

Oh, I can't stand her. What a wuss.

Lunilla sniffs. "That's kind of hard to accept. At any time, one of you could raise an army against me."

"I wouldn't need an army," Snowy says. There's an edge to her voice and my hopes perk up. "I could have taken back the palace a long time ago, with my magic. But I don't want it, none of us do."

"Speak for yourself," I say.

Both Snowy and Lunilla give me savage glares.

"It's my palace," I say. "My father was King Edgar. There's not a reason in the world why that lady should be queen."

"Be quiet!" Snowy says. Lunilla's face has gone red. Good! If she's mad, maybe she'll try to attack me. Or Snowy. And then Snowy can blast her with ice.

Beauty rolls her eyes. "Oh sure, like *you'd* be the queen. Let's put the kingdom in the hands of a kitten, that's a good idea."

"I'm not a kitten!"

"Silence, both of you!" Snowy shouts. "We're leaving! And none of us are ever coming back!"

"I can't accept that," Lunilla says.

"You're hardly in a position to argue!" Snowy says.

"What, you think I'm powerless?" Lunilla says. "Tell me, can you really protect these girls? Every day, all the time? Perhaps you've forgotten about my precious pet. Believe me, sooner or later, he'll find them."

Snowy straightens her posture. Her face goes blank. I begin to hear little ticks of sound and feel something cold pecking my skin. Beads of ice drop and bounce off the floor – tiny hailstones. Within seconds, they grow to the size of fingertips and a clattering storm of hail rains down on the throne room, battering the marble floor and spraying us with droplets of water. Lunilla screams and Cooper throws himself on top of her. Beauty and I crouch and cover our heads. The rush of falling ice is deafening, the stones pummel my back and spine, but underneath it, my heart is cheering. Go Snowy! Crush them all!

The shower rattles to a stop. Slowly, we all stand up.

Snowy folds her arms. "That was a demonstration. I could've dropped boulders on your heads. Can't release your precious pet if you're dead, can you?"

Lunilla cowers in her chair, the hailstones sunk into the puffs and folds of her dress. "You – you don't know where it lives." She's still trying to fight back. "I already gave it – it has the girls' scents. It could find them on its own."

"I want the Beast slain," Snowy says. "At once. Bring it here and I'll do it myself."

"We can't bring it," Cooper says, brushing bits of ice off his sleeves. The floor has become a carpet of white stones, we can't even move without kicking them. "We can barely control it as it is."

"Then take me to it," Snowy says.

"No!" Lunilla scrambles up from her chair. "Listen, just take away the cold weather. That's all we want. And I'll make sure the Beast doesn't harm the girls. You wanted something peaceful, right?"

"Yeah, come on, Snowy," Cooper says. "No need for this all to get ugly. We'll leave the girls alone if you get rid of the snow. It's that simple."

"No, I want the Beast slain," Snowy says.

"Or she'll slay you all!" I say, grinning.

Snowy whirls around to glare at me but her eyes find something else. I turn and look. Kay has come into the throne room from a doorway near the front. He strides toward us, crunching hailstones under his books, and points at Snowy. "There she is!"

In a blink, Godnutter is next to him. Just appears on the spot. She thrusts out her arm and aims her pipe at Snowy. A stream of white sparkles shoots out of the tip and hits Snowy in the chest. She gasps. The sparkles seem to enter her body, her skin glows from inside like a lantern. She shrieks, arches back, and her hands are jerked outward. From each palm, the sparkles fly out again, but this time they're blue. Like ribbons of light, they flow out of her and there's a rush of icy wind as they pass me. The sparkles are sucked across the room and back into the tip of Godnutter's pipe.

Chapter 29

Snowy is hunched over, staring at her hands. She's panting.

"What did you do?" I ask Godnutter.

"It's gone," Snowy whispers. "Oh my stars, it's gone."

"What's gone?" I ask.

Godnutter cackles. "The Snow Queen is gone. She's only Snow White now. Boring little Snow White."

Lunilla's eyes widen. "You took her magic?"

"Every last morsel of it." Godnutter smirks. "Been meaning to do that for ages."

"Why?" Snowy cries.

"It was your fault my Cindy got cursed," Godnutter says. "I left you alone to raise her daughter - figured you needed the magic to keep her safe. But when smiley guy here discovered the girl, I decided the time had come to get even. He was good enough to cooperate with me."

We all look at Kay. He looks tense but speaks in a quiet voice. "The Ice Witch had to be stopped. She made life harsh for everyone in the kingdom. The old fairy told me that if I got Zelly out and brought her to the palace, it would free her up to defeat the Ice Witch."

"What?" I say.

Kay lifts his hands. "We're still friends, Zelly. It was nothing against you. You weren't happy living with Snow White, you told me that."

"I don't care!" I shout. "You can't just do that!" I feel like he's kicked me in the stomach. I feel like I'm going to throw up.

"Oh, but we did." Godnutter snaps her fingers over the pipe and brings it to her lips. Little curls of gray rise out of the bowl. "I told the boy to bring the redhaired girl to the palace and then summon me when the Snow Brat came to fetch her. I wanted to do this in front of everyone.

Lunilla has begun to smile. "Well, look at you, Kay. That was pretty dark. I'm surprised at you; you never seemed to mind the cold weather so much."

"No, but Beauty did," Kay says.

I gasp. I honestly want to wring his neck. "This was all for HER?"

Beauty shakes her head at Kay. "You're crazy. You're demented. Do you really think this is going to change anything?"

"But you said...." Kay rushes to her, scattering hailstones, and seizes her hands. "You said if I did something heroic, you'd take me seriously. The winter will end now, you can have your rose garden."

"*You* didn't do that!" Beauty yanks back her hands. "Godnutter did! Getting someone to do the work for you isn't my idea of a hero."

"Oh, come on, Beauty!" Kay cries.

"Nope, sorry. You'll have to do better than that." She strokes back her hair and turns away from Kay, a faint smile tweaking her lips. She's enjoying his anguish.

Kay looks struck. He stares at her, pale and hopeless, arms hanging limp at his sides. Despite my anger at him, I'm now furious with Beauty. How could she refuse him? How could she hurt him like that? I would not have hurt him for the world.

"Go upstairs, Kay," Lunilla says with false sweetness. "Have a talk with Mama if you think it will help."

Kay leaves the ballroom without looking at me once. He looks miserable. I'm hurting for him. But I'm hurting even more for myself.

Snowy is still bent over, staring at her hands. Her black hair has slipped forward and hangs in her face. We all just stand there - watching her - and it feels very awkward. Cooper clears his throat.

"So, what happens now?" he says.

Godnutter blows out a gray cloud and smiles. "Now I throw you both out of the palace."

Lunilla gasps.

Godnutter chuckles. "Oh, not yet, dumpling! Not yet. But listen!" She points her pipe at Lunilla like a scolding finger. "I disabled the Snow Queen for you. Now you owe me a favor. These girls are true princesses and they've been in exile. Now that they're nearly of age, it's time they returned to their rightful home at the palace." Her voice hardens. "You will let them stay."

Lunilla has a way of puffing up when she's angry. That's what she looks like now, a bird with its feathers all fluffed out. "I don't have to honor that."

"We can't stay here!" Beauty cries. "She'll feed us to the Beast, she said that!"

"Huh. Forgot about him." Godnutter says it like the Beast is no big deal. "He's probably gotten pretty feral by now, hasn't he?"

Lunilla shrugs. "He does act... beastly."

"Where you keeping him?" Godnutter asks.

"That's my business," Lunilla says.

Godnutter snorts and smoke bursts from her nostrils. "I bet you have him right here. In the palace." Her eyes travel to the ceiling. "I could find him pretty quick, if I wanted to."

"It's not here," Cooper says. "I'm being honest. Her sister didn't want it here, she was afraid for Kay. And we have the baby. We told the guards not to let it near the palace."

"So where is it?" Godnutter says.

"You really don't know?" Beauty says.

"I'm a fairy, not some kind of goddess," Godnutter says. "I don't know everything. But you know what? I'm not worried."

"Why?" Lunilla says.

"Well, you're not smart, Loony, but you're not too stupid either. If any harm came to these girls, I think you know what would happen."

Lunilla turns red. "You'd come after me?"

Godnutter gives a snappy headshake. "Oh, not you, honeybun. Someone much smaller."

Cooper growls. "She means Jack!"

"I know she means Jack!" Lunilla snaps. She folds her arms and turns back to Godnutter. Her face has begun to sweat. "All right, fine! The girls can stay."

Godnutter nods. "And let me be clear, they're not your prisoners. This is their home, now. You will give them a room and treat them fairly. The redhead will probably need a good education and definitely a haircut. And Beauty needs to learn how to be queen."

"What?" Lunilla and Beauty cry.

"Oh, I'm sorry. Did you still think I'd let your beanie boy have the throne? Not a chance, baby doll. This is Cinderella's castle and until her return, her daughter will serve as queen. It's only right. But I'm willing to make a deal with you. Why don't we marry your Kay to my Beauty? They'll make a decent king and queen."

This pretty much makes everyone furious. Lunilla refuses to give up the throne. Beauty refuses to marry Kay. And I'm completely ignored. I glower at Godnutter, waving her pipe around as she speaks. This isn't fair. Just because she has magic doesn't mean she can do whatever she wants. If someone took that pipe away, could she really boss us around like this?

Cooper stands by Lunilla with his arm around her. "Look," he says to Godnutter. "You're asking too much. The palace was empty, it was up for grabs. Lunilla and I took it for ourselves, fair and square. You can't just kick us out."

"The people won't like it!" Lunilla shouts. "Nearly everyone in this kingdom has known only ME as their queen. They don't know about Cinderella's daughters. If you switch queens on them, they're going to riot all over again!"

"And what about the fairies?" I say to Godnutter. "What if they don't agree with this idea? Snowy says they don't like you too much."

Godnutter shrugs. "They don't. But they don't like Loony much either, especially with her habit of killing young, innocent girls. They weren't able to save them all and that's rankled. They tolerate the queen but I'm sure a replacement would be welcome. Might even put me back into their good graces! I'm returning the baby I stole."

"What about the curse?" I say.

"I'm getting to that!" Godnutter yanks the pipe out of her mouth and gives me a nasty look. I get the feeling I'm not her favorite. "I've been reading my spell books. I found one – and only one - that may help us. There's an immunity spell for newly-crowned queens that will shield them from curses and even cancel those already cast. I'm working on mixing it up for Beauty but it'll take me..." she holds up three fingers at Lunilla "...three days. And that's counting today! So pack your bags, take the baby, and find yourself a cozy cottage. And don't try anything funny. Because in three days, I'm coming back here and we are crowning Beauty as queen."

And she vanishes.

Chapter 30

There's nothing more to say. Lunilla stands beside Cooper, her large chest heaving. I'm near Snowy, who looks like a wilted flower. She lifts her face and her eyes have changed. They're like black holes, empty and lost. "Cooper, can you take me to my room? My old room? I won't bother anyone there."

"Where is it?" Cooper asks.

"At the top of one of the towers," Snowy says. "It's small."

Lunilla flicks out a hand. "Take her, Coop. I'm not sure what I should do with her, I didn't receive *instructions* on that one. Just get her out of here."

"Will do," Cooper says.

"And *I'm* going to the garden," Lunilla says, sloshing through hailstones that have mostly melted by now. "And NOBODY better speak to me for a VERY long time!" Clenching her fists, she marches from the throne room.

Cooper lays a hand on Snowy's shoulder. "Come on, girl." Without pushing or hurrying her, he leads her away. There's no one left but me and Beauty.

Beauty stands with a hand on her hip, looking generally annoyed. Like she hasn't just been told she's going to be queen in three days.

"So... we're staying here?" I say.

"That seems to be the plan." Beauty flips back her hair. "Would've been nice if she asked what *we* wanted to do. But overall, I guess it's not bad."

"Are we princesses now?"

"Ugh! I can't deal with you." Beauty spreads out her hands in frustration and walks away from me.

I hurry to catch up with her. "Where are you going?"

"To have a bath," Beauty says.

I look back at my braid, bedraggled and dirty. After that filthy dungeon, it's not a bad idea.

We manage to find a servant, who takes us to another servant, who take us to the housekeeper. She's a stout woman with a frowning mouth but she's actually pretty nice. Our scene in the throne room, she tells us, was witnessed by a few servants who huddled behind doorways to watch. I guess the sound of an indoor hailstorm would draw a few curious eyes, right?

The housekeeper leads us to the upper floors of the palace, explaining that although she has not received specific orders from the queen, she can at least make us comfortable.

"Do you want separate rooms or together?" the housekeeper asks. Beauty and I glance at each other.

"Separate," we both say.

The room she gives me is huge and square, so unlike my tower in every way that for five minutes, I stand there and wonder at it. The walls are blue, with white birds painted on them. The furniture is so shiny I can see my face in it. There are large paintings of forests and animals and strange ladies sitting in chairs. And my bed has its own roof.

I have absolutely no idea what I should do. But I'm saved by two ladies who appear at the door, introduce themselves as servants, and say they are here to help me. I mumble something about washing my hair. They take me through another door and I discover that I also have a room just for taking baths, with a large copper tub which I'm told to stand in. What follows is pretty much the most embarrassing hour of my life. Those two servant ladies simply yank off my clothes like there's nothing weird about that and begin to scrub down both me and my hair. They think my hair is funny and laugh over it a lot, making jokes I don't understand. To be fair, though, they wash it a lot faster than Snowy does.

Afterwards, I sit in my new room and wait for my cheeks to stop burning. I'm next to an open window and the air that slides over me is... warm. Water drips onto the outer sill from somewhere higher up on the castle.

The kingdom is losing its winter. Somehow, that makes me really sad.

"Zelly?"

I turn my head, but carefully. The two servant ladies put three chairs behind me and sort of bridged my hair across them to help it dry. Kay leans in at the doorway to my room, holding up a silver goblet. "I brought you some water," he says.

"I thought a prince didn't fetch water."

Kay grins. "Just this once... again." He steps across the room and hands me the goblet. I take a sip and then lower the cup to my lap.

"May I sit?" Kay points at a bench along the wall by my window. I nod.

"I like your dress," Kay says. The two servant ladies took away my warm blue dress for washing and brought me a smooth gown of deep russet red. It's a little big – the sleeves almost cover my hands – but I like it.

"Thanks," I say.

Kay sniffs and rubs his nose. His eyes have a slight puffiness to them and I wonder if he's been crying. He glances at my hair trailing over the chairs behind me. "Hey, I like your hair like that. All loose."

"I can't braid it until it's dry," I say. "The two servant ladies said they'd come back and do it for me." I cup my hands around the goblet in my lap. "Do I, um, have to keep them?"

Kay gives a laugh. "You're a princess now. Servants are a necessary nuisance."

"Do you have them?"

"Just one, really, who waits on me. He's been with me since I was ten, he's like a friend now."

"Servants can be friends?" I didn't know that. I was too nervous with the servant ladies to talk to them. They weren't much older than me, I think. Maybe I should try. When they come back, I will ask them their names.

Kay sighs. "Zelly, I owe you an apology. I never should've left you alone with the queen. I didn't know she was going to throw you in prison but I should've guessed she had bad intentions. I didn't believe her at all when she said you got sick and went home."

"The dungeon stank," I say.

"You should never have gone there. You know, I'm actually glad Aunt Lunilla is getting replaced. She was never a good queen, it's time we had a new one."

I smirk. "Especially if it's Beauty."

"I didn't say that."

"You don't have to." I give him a stern look. "Did you really conspire with the wicked fairy to trick me out of my tower?"

Kay lowers his head. "It wasn't my idea. It was your music that led me to you, that wasn't a lie. Then the old fairy appeared to me in The Wood. All she wanted was that I bring you to the palace by persuasion and not by force. She thought it would be nicer that way. We did want to stop the Ice Witch and I couldn't tell you that but it wasn't an evil scheme. I'm not a bad person."

I snort. Funny how people say that when they do something wrong. It doesn't excuse what he did to Snowy. Or me. I trace my thumb over the rim of my goblet and chew on my next words before saying them.

"We're... we're not really friends, are we Kay?"

"What? Sure we are! Of course, we are!"

I shake my head. "I heard that friends are always there for you. But you're not. You're always going to leave me and run back to Beauty."

"If – if she would just... accept me!" Kay says, opening his hands. "Then we'd be fine – you and I, I mean. I just can't focus on anything else, right now. I know I sound crazy but I really do love her, Zelly."

"Why?"

Kay rakes back his hair. "She's just so...."

I wait a few seconds. "Beautiful?"

"Not just that," Kay says.

"No, I think it *is* just that." And it feels wrong. In my books, the pretty girls were always nice. But Beauty isn't. I think niceness should be more important.

"You know it was... a real shocker, finding out you two are sisters," Kay says. "And when I look at you now, I can see it. You both blink the same and have the same teeth. I'm glad you found each other, I think it's great."

Ugh. I don't.

Kay shifts closer to me. "But since you *are* sisters, do you think... do you think you could talk to her about me? She might listen to you-"

"What?" I try to stand but the weight of my wet hair tugs me down. I hit the chair hard and slosh water onto my dress.

"Get out of here!" I shout.

"Why?" he cries.

"Just GET OUT!" I point my whole arm at the door and leave it there until Kay shuffles out of the room.

I hunch over my lap and cry. He's not my friend. He's never going to *be* my friend. All because of stupid Beauty. Tears spill off my cheeks and into my lap. A few of them drop into my goblet of water. It doesn't matter. Snowy can't freeze them or sell them anymore. She can't do anything.

It's all a waste.

Chapter 31

I want to see Snowy, I have stuff to talk about. But I don't know where her room is. And I can't move from this chair for at least another two hours. My hair is really annoying me right now. It was fine in the tower but in a huge palace like this... it might not work.

I stare out the window while the sun is setting and watch the fire-gold clouds slowly cool into purple evening. The snow on the ground is sparkly, a sure sign it's melting. The two servant ladies come back and talk in happy tones about the change in weather. They split my hair into five sections and start weaving from the top of my head. I end up with the fanciest braid I ever had, twice as wide as my normal one and much shorter. It still drags the ground, but not nearly as much.

I can finally stand up. "Where's Snowy?" I ask. They have no idea who I'm talking about until I say, 'The Ice Witch.' One of them jabbers through a list of directions I can't possibly understand but I'm too embarrassed to say so. I leave the room with only a vague idea of 'left' and 'up.'

I carry the end of my thick, fancy braid in one hand and my goblet of water in the other. I feel like I should ask Snowy about the tears. It's probably pointless now, but I hate to just throw them away.

I turn left and walk for a while. I climb some stairs and walk a while more. It's all the same, just hallways and doors. I don't see any people at all. What do I do? How will I ever find my room again? What if I'm lost up here forever?

I hear a cough – and know who it is. I whirl around to listen. It's not far, I trace the sound to a door maybe ten steps back. She's still coughing. I hover outside the room, hesitant, then I turn the handle and let myself in.

It's another large bedroom. The walls are pale gray and the furniture is made of natural wood and doesn't shine. Melodie is sitting on her wide bed with a blanket over her legs. She looks surprised to see me.

"Do you know where Snowy's room is?" I ask.

Melodie tries to speak but her voice crackles and she coughs again. She grabs a small pitcher off the table by her bed and spits into it. Panting, she puts the pitcher back.

"I'm sorry," she whispers. "It hurts so much."

"What hurts?"

Melodie takes a few deep breaths. "My chest. My throat. Feels like it's choking me." She coughs again, ending with gags, and I hear the phlegm inside her. When she grabs the spit pitcher, I turn my face away. It's too gross.

"I'm sorry," she says again.

She looks awful. Pale and weak, with dark rings around her eyes. She's still wearing her nightdress and her hair is loose and stringy. I don't think she got up today.

"Are you always like this?" I ask.

"I have good days and bad days," she says. Her voice is scratchy. "But as the years go by, the bad days come more often. I'm so tired...." She slumps back on the bed and tries in vain to clear her throat.

"Do you need some water?" I ask.

"I drank it all," Melodie says.

Oh my blood and bones. I just thought of something. But wait, should I do it? Yes... I should. But she has to pay me first. That's what Snowy said, she always made the people pay first.

"Where's Snowy's room?" I ask again.

"You mean the one she grew up in?"

"I think so."

Melodie has another coughing fit before continuing. "Go up one floor. Find the painting of a castle on a glass hill. The door to her tower will be beside it."

I nod. Payment accepted.

"Here." I offer her the goblet of water, half-filled, lukewarm, and holding my two dissolved tears. "This is from Kay."

"From Kay?" Melodie reaches for it.

I nod. Melodie takes a small sip and leans over to put the cup on her bedside table.

"Oh, um… you need to drink it all," I say. "Kay thinks you need it. I want to tell him you drank the whole thing. I mean, there's not much in there."

"All right. Wish he brought it to me himself, though." Melodie returns the cup to her lips. I watch her tip it back until I'm sure she has swallowed all of the water.

"Thank you." She hands me the cup.

"I'll let you rest now," I say.

But I leave the room with a huge grin on my face. By tomorrow morning, she'll have no cough at all. It will never come back.

Because my tears have healing magic. They can cure any sickness.

And oh, excuse me, can *Beauty* do that?

Chapter 32

I find Snowy's room. It's at the top of a winding staircase, cramped and dark. I step around chunks of broken candles littering the stairs. When she doesn't answer my knock, I let myself in.

The room is small and round. It feels like home. Looks like it hasn't been used in years; it's mostly bare, dingy with dust, and the bed doesn't even have sheets on it. Snowy's sitting on the floor underneath the one window, her right side pressed to the wall. Her knees are drawn up, her face bowed over them.

I pull the rest of my braid into the room and shut the door. "Hey, Snowy."

She doesn't move.

There's a chair by her bed. I drag it forward and sit on it. "This was your room? It doesn't look... princessy."

"Cinderella put me here," Snowy says. "She wanted me out of the way."

"You don't have to stay here. There are other rooms, really nice ones. I think you can stay where you want."

Snowy shakes her head.

I don't like seeing her this way. She looks small and girlish. She's thrown her black cloak into a corner and just sits there in her white wool dress. Like a little mound of snow, ready to melt away.

"Snowy...."

"Why did you leave?" she asks without lifting her head. "You ruined everything. We're finished now."

"I wanted to see people," I say. "I couldn't stay there forever, Snowy. It wasn't fair."

"Nothing is fair," Snowy says. "But we were safe. And now it's all over." She moans and looks at her hands. "My magic is *gone*, Rapunzel, do you understand? I have nothing left."

I frown. "You have me."

"You left me!" Snowy says, turning hot eyes on me. "Did you even think about my feelings? I was frantic when I came home and couldn't find you. Did you think about that?"

"They threw me in prison! I couldn't help it!"

"You could if you hadn't left at all."

Ugh! I stand up and pace around. She never tries to understand. "Well, I'm sorry but we're not dead! You just lost your magic, that's all. I know you're going to miss it but you didn't always have it, right?"

"I got it the day I lost Hunter." Snowy leans her head into the wall and shuts her eyes. "Hunter made me feel special. The magic made me feel strong. And now I feel nothing, I *am* nothing. I may as well die."

I stop by the window, sighing. It's a narrow window but taller than I am. I find a latch on one side and nudge it open to bring some air into this musty room. Directly below is the rose garden, looking very small from here. I should probably tell Snowy that Hunter is alive. But I'm nervous about it. Either she'll freak out or she won't believe me at all. If she does believe me, she'll want to see him and I don't know how to make him come. Still... I guess I should tell her.

"I – I don't think it's the end, Snowy," I say. "I think we can start a new life here. You might even be happy again, because-"

"Lunilla is going to kill us," Snowy says. "Don't think for a moment that she won't. You, me, Beauty – we're all dead. Godnutter's threat is just an obstacle, there are ways to get around it. I don't know Lunilla but I know her type and they don't lose gracefully. All she has to do is have one of the fairies hide her baby. And we are dead."

My chest tightens. "But...."

"So, congratulate yourself, Rapunzel." Snowy looks at me and her eyes are black as a starless night. "You'll see your coffin before your sixteenth birthday. I hope you're very proud."

Tears flood into my eyes. "Fine! I hope the Beast eats your first!" I yank up my braid and leave, sobbing by the time I'm midway down the stairs. I hate Snowy! I hate her so much!

I try to find my room again but in my anger, I'm not paying much attention. The palace just seems to go on and on, another turn, another wing, another tower. I don't know why it has to be so big. I think I found my floor - at least, the paintings look familiar. I pass a room with an open door and hear someone humming inside. It sounds like Beauty, slightly off-key. But when I peek in, I don't see her.

I rub my eyes with my sleeve and walk in. She has a sunny room of yellow and white, with shiny furniture like mine. But unlike mine, there's a set of glass doors that go outside. When I look out, I gasp and step back. Beauty is sitting in a kind of outdoor room with a low fence around it. Strange enough but that's not what made me gasp. She's perched on a low stool and working at a device. A wooden device with a wheel that spins.

I push open the glass door. "What's that?"

Beauty doesn't act surprised to see me at all. "It's a spinning wheel. Never saw one?"

"Beauty! What about the curse?"

"The curse is on my birthday," she says. "I can spin all I want until then. I need to make a dress."

"A dress?"

"For my coronation." Beauty smiles and it's way too smug. "Now watch this. Are you watching?"

I fold my arms. "Yes."

Beauty pumps a wide pedal with her foot and sets the wheel spinning. She's got a bundle of straw in her lap and feeds it onto a thread that runs through a small hole in the device and gets wrapped around a spool. The spool stands on a slender spike that points upward. That must be it: the spindle.

"Look closely," Beauty says. She adds another bit of straw to the thread and pinches it between her fingers. Her fingers slide back, twisting the straw around the thread. I wash her pinch and slide, pinch and slide, adding more straw as she goes. As it passes between her fingers, I'm surprised by a flash of brilliance.

"Is that...?" I look at the spool, filling with new string. It doesn't look like straw anymore. It's smooth and shining and almost looks like-

"Gold?" I say.

Beauty grins. "I can spin straw into gold. Real gold! I always could, it's my little magic trick. How about you, got any magic tricks?"

"My tears can heal the sick," I say.

Beauty snorts. "That's not much, the fairies do things like that. But I'm the only one who can make gold from plain straw. I discovered it when I was little."

"Me too," I say.

"I need a new dress. The most magnificent one I've ever had. Godnutter can make the dress for me but I have to provide the gold. I'll need about twelve large spools, I think. That's why I have to get started."

"You had on a gold dress at the party," I say. "Why can't you use that?"

"That's my second gold dress," Beauty says. "I won't destroy it to make this one, they're part of my collection. I'll be the golden queen."

I roll my eyes. The spinning wheel whirs as she continues to pump the pedal. Beyond the stone fence, night is descending and the land is darkening to cool patches of blue.

"What are we standing on?" I ask.

Beauty laughs. "It's a balcony! Goodness, Zelly, you don't know anything!"

I flinch. "Don't call me that."

"Why not? Kay does."

"It's just for him."

"Aw, that's sweet." Beauty grins at me. "You really like him, don't you, Zelly?"

I clench my fists. "Why don't *you* like him? You're really hurting him with this. He just wants you to give him a chance." I'm not really arguing for Kay. I just want to know why.

"He's too nice." Beauty grabs more straw from a bundle by her feet and lays it across her lap. "Nice is boring. I don't want to be just a pretty girl with a nice husband. It's too ordinary."

"Kay's not ordinary."

164

"I don't need him! I can be queen by myself," Beauty says. "I don't want him to be the king, that's giving him exactly what he wants."

"He wants it?"

Beauty smirks. "He wasn't too happy when little Jack was born. Tries to hide his disappointment but I can tell. Kay was first in line to be king until then. And now he's not." She stands up and leans back to stretch her back. She walks to the front of the balcony and rests her hands on the stone railing. "Besides, Kay is just a boy. I could have any man I wanted."

I follow her, frowning. "What do you mean, he's just a boy? What kind of...." I feel myself blushing. "What kind of... *man* do you like, if you don't like Kay?"

Beauty's face changes. Her pristine profile droops a little, her lashes falter. "Leave me alone."

I have a hunch. Because she looks like Snowy when she's talking about Hunter. With a smirk, I lean closer. "What's wrong, Beauty? Is there someone out there who doesn't like *you?*"

Beauty turns and smacks my face.

I gasp and step back, covering my stinging cheek. "You hit me!"

Beauty shoves her hands against my chest and I fall backward, my braid just saving my hip from the stone floor. When I try to scramble up, she steps on my braid.

"Forgetting your manners, little girl?" she snarls.

I yank my braid out from under her foot, jump up and run. She chases me as far as the bedroom door but when I'm tearing down the hall, I don't hear her behind me. She yells something that sounds mean but I can't make out the words.

I take all the stairs I can find that lead downward. Eventually, I burst out of the castle and into the rose garden. I'm sobbing and there's no one – not Snowy, not Kay, not anybody – to comfort me. I trudge down the nearest path, crying through clenched teeth, so angry that I grab random roses off the bushes and hurl them at the ground, petals spraying.

Snowy never hit me. Other than her accidental ice blast the other day, she never tried to hurt me. Beauty just smacked my face! I burn all over with the shame of it, cry in angry heaves. My face is who I am. It's what makes me Rapunzel and not someone else. I feel like all of me was hit, my whole person. My whole me.

I stop walking because my hand hurts. I uncurl my fist and find a bleeding puncture wound on my first finger and some scratches from when I grabbed the roses off the bushes. I forgot about the thorns.

I stare at the wound on my hand and my eyes slide up the palace wall. Beauty's probably still up there, spinning at her stupid wheel, so confident she's going to escape the curse. But I know one thing about that curse that she doesn't. And it's going to be her downfall.

She's never going to have Kay. She's never going to be the queen. And she's *never* going to hit me again.

You will prick your friggin' finger, Beauty. And I will make it happen.

Chapter 33

I find a bench made of curling iron and sit down. I pull the sleeve of my dress over the wound until the bleeding stops. Gradually, my sniffling subsides.

I hear a door slam, a voice shouting. And I groan. Lunilla is coming.

"I want them dead, I want them all dead! Right now! All of them!" She comes into view and marches up a path with Cooper behind her. "There has to be a way!"

"I'm thinking, I just don't know," he says.

"You're not with me on this!" Lunilla whirls around and points in his face. "You're soft on the Ice Witch, I can see it!"

"Look, Snowy's no threat to us," Cooper says. "We should let her go home, she seems pretty broken anyway. It's those girls that are the problem."

At this point, they both see me. We're separated by only a few rows of bushes and I wasn't trying to hide. I'm disappointed, though - I liked watching them fight.

"Hello," I say.

"What're you doing there?" Cooper barks.

"Just sitting. What are you doing?"

"We're trying to get rid of you!" Lunilla says.

I nod. "I can see that. This is like your worst nightmare, isn't it?"

"Don't get cocky," Lunilla says. "I'm not worried about *you*. You're the least important one here."

I lift my chin. "I'm more important than you think."

"Ugh, she is SO like her mother! That was Cindy all over again, always had something to prove."

"I think the other one's like Cinderella," Cooper says. "Plain nasty."

"It's the fairy we need to worry about," Lunilla says. "She's the one tying our hands. If we stop the fairy, we stop them all."

"I don't know how," Cooper says. "She's got too much magic. She can do whatever she wants."

"What about the roses?" Lunilla gestures at the shrubs around her. "The blue ones make you forget everything. Maybe we could put it in her tea."

"She won't fall for that," I say. "You're better off just taking her pipe away."

Lunilla stares at me. She turns and looks at Cooper with wide eyes.

"I don't know..." he says.

"But Coop! All of her spells are stored in that pipe. If we could steal it-"

"She'll still have magic without it. She's a fairy," Cooper says.

"But that pipe is her weapon, her magic wand. She wouldn't want to lose it. It's something to think about, at least."

I stand up. I wasn't really serious but they're taking it that way. There's no way anyone could steal that pipe. Except Beauty... maybe. But I doubt Godnutter leaves it lying around.

I walk around a corner of the castle wall with a vague idea of going back inside. I'm still in the garden, which is spacious and sprawling, like everything else at this palace. Once I'm sure Lunilla can't see me, I stop and pluck a blue rose off one of the bushes, breaking the stem with my thumbnail. I twirl the blossom in my fingers but don't touch the petals. The blue roses make you forget, she said. There's something I like about that.

My shoulders tense up. Something is wrong. I spin around, expecting someone behind me but no one is there. I don't hear Lunilla's voice anymore – maybe she went inside. I glance at the palace and my eyes travel up the wall to a slender tower far above me. I squint my eyes and step back.

There's a window near the top of the tower, tall and narrow. A woman stands at the window, looking out – no wait, she's standing *on* the window. Right on the sill, her hands gripping the walls, her white dress flapping in the breeze.

It's Snowy.

What's she doing? That's dangerous! Why would she climb out onto the ledge, is she looking for something? I can't make out her face, but she's not looking down. She simply stares ahead of her. And then she takes her hands off the sides of the window and covers her face.

And Snowy steps off the sill.

Chapter 34

My whole body jerks and I scream like mad. Snowy drops like a stone in front of the palace, twirling end over end, her face hidden beneath her hands. In two seconds, she's halfway to the ground, in three seconds-

A blast of light shoots at the palace. It seems to dive from the sky and aim at Snowy. The light hits her with an exploding flash of gold and a boom that knocks me to the ground. I roll to my side and stare with huge eyes. The light rises momentarily above the garden and then begins to lower itself. The blinding glow shrinks until, finally, I can see what's behind it. It's the fairy, Hunter. With Snowy in his arms.

I hear Snowy's shriek of disbelief. "HUNTER!"

His face is tense. He floats down the few remaining feet to the ground, his silvery wings fanned out. Though he sets Snowy down carefully, her limbs collapse like a newborn deer and she turns her eyes up to Hunter as if terrified. "HUNTER!"

"Shhh... it's me, Snowy, it's me." He crouches and takes her face in his hands. "It's all right, don't be afraid. I couldn't let you harm yourself, I couldn't do that." His eyebrows curl upward, he looks shaken.

"Hunter?" Snowy's hands shake as she reaches for him. She touches his cheeks with her fingertips, curves her hands over the line of his jaw. For a long moment, they simply gaze at each other, each one holding the other's face. I can't even breathe as I watch them.

"I am so sorry, my Snow Queen," Hunter says in a voice so soft and beautiful, I creep forward on my elbows to hear better. I fell beside a stretch of blue rose bushes and I shuffle closer to them to conceal myself.

"What happened?" Snowy asks. She moves her hands to Hunter's shoulders but seems afraid to let go of him. "I – I saw you die! I saw it, Hunter, the Mirror killed you. I was right there!"

"I know. It was horrible." He brushes her cheek with the backs of his fingers. "It was the fairies, Snowy. They saved me. Although my body had been destroyed, my life essence clung to it, just faintly. But it was enough for them. The only way to save me was to make me one of their own."

Snowy gasps. "I – I've heard of that! Cinderella once said-"

Hunter nods. "Yes. It was done for her godmother. Not everyone is given that chance, they have to consider you worth saving. And they struggled with me. I was kept in heavy sleep while they worked their spells on me but I nearly slipped away a few times. My healing took over a year."

"A year...." Snowy looks at him and her eyes, for a moment, turn reproachful. "But – but afterward. When you woke up...."

Hunter sighs. "I know. I wasn't sure what to do. I wanted to show you I was alive, but...." He takes her hands and gently squeezes her fingers. "I thought I'd be breaking your heart all over. To come and see you... and then leave you again.... We couldn't go back to what we were, Snowy, too much had happened. Our paths had turned in different directions. I wanted you to be free, to move on with your life."

"But I didn't! I can't!" Snowy says, her voice rising to a tearful pitch. "I never stopped mourning for you! Every day my heart *ached* until I felt like it would split open. I can't forget you, Hunter! You were my first love."

Hunter gives her his dazzling smiling. "And you were mine. That's never going to change. But the heart has many chambers, Snowy. There is room for so much love. Keep me in one of your chambers and I'll always keep you in one of mine. But clear a space for someone else."

Snowy wipes her eyes and I think she's going to sob. But when she looks at Hunter, she smiles. "I'm so glad you're alive. And that you don't blame me for what happened."

"Not at all," he says softly.

"May I hug you?"

"Of course."

Still on their knees, they clutch each other so tightly, I can't even see their faces. He got a hand pressed to the back of her head; her arms cross behind him and she clenches his tunic with both fists. It seems a long time before they let go.

Snowy wipes away more tears but when she looks at him, she laughs. "This might sound a little strange but... you look so young!"

Hunter laughs. "Nineteen. That's it for me."

"Do I look much different to you?"

He tilts his head and pretends to study her. "A little less girlish. A lot more beautiful." He smiles. "But... also less joyful, I think."

Snowy lowers her head and nods. "It's been hard. I felt very much alone. I lost everyone, even...." She looks up again. "Oh my stars, what about your brothers? Do they know you're alive?"

"Yes, I made sure of that. When they saw me, they were immensely relieved. It broke the grudge they had against you, they stopped trying to hunt you down. That was important to me, I wanted you safe."

Snowy looks pouty. "I still think you should've told me. I was in my tower all that time...." She gasps and covers her mouth. "Oh! What about Cinderella? You said... I thought... why haven't you kissed her awake?"

I twitch in my spot beneath the bushes. That's a good question.

Hunter sighs. "It's tragic that she's been asleep for so long. But I can't break the curse. I'm no longer fully human, I'm part spirit now, like all fairies. But I do feel that someone will come for her. For her sake, I hope so."

"Ooh! Wait! I have a question!" I scramble up to my feet. Snowy looks shocked to see me but Hunter does not. I think he knew I was there all along.

I hurry up to them. "Snowy, I'm... I'm sorry but I saw you fall. I was right over there." I point behind me.

Snowy shakes her head. "No, it was my fault. I did an extremely foolish thing. I felt...." She shuts her eyes. "It won't happen again, I'm sorry."

I look down, feeling embarrassed. It's not like her to apologize. "I'd like to ask Hunter something, if that's all right."

Snowy nods and steps back. Hunter smiles and his soft brown eyes are so beautiful, it makes me shiver.

"You knew my mother, right?" I say.

"I did."

I blink fast and feel the beginnings of tears. "Could you tell me something nice about her? No one ever says anything nice about her."

"Well, how strange, because she had such beautiful qualities. She always spoke to me with respect and her voice was soft and elegant. She had a touching devotion to the memory of her father and told me lovely stories

176

about him. And when her babies were born, she held them and sang to them with so much joy in her face. She loved her children."

I'm crying. Not openly but my face is all scrunched and the tears pour down. "Thank you," I say, wiping my cheeks with my sleeves. "That's – that's good."

"I'm sorry you never knew her. It wasn't supposed to be this way, you should have grown up with your mother and your twin sister."

It's only because I like him that I don't scoff at this. I'm glad I didn't grow up with Beauty!

Hunter turns back to Snowy. "Come, I'll take you home. You'll be happier there, you always liked that tower."

"Thank you," Snowy says. "Could you also bring Rapunzel? She should go home, too."

"No, I want to stay here," I say.

"Rapunzel," Snowy says.

I shake my head. "No. I'm sick of that tower. I want to stay here and be a princess."

"It's not safe," Snowy says.

"Here. Maybe I can help." Hunter takes out a wand from inside his tunic. He clasps my shoulder with one hand and with the other, touches the wand to the top of my head.

He whispers a few words and a sensation of warmth slides through me. It's very exciting!

"What did you do?" I ask.

"An enchantment. A small one," Hunter says. "It'll keep you safe from magic spells for a few days. Just in case Lunilla tries to poison you with her roses or God-nutter aims her pipe at you. But it's not permanent, those spells are a lot of work. I'll come back in a few days and check on you."

I nod, grinning. I like being spelled on.

Snowy's face droops a little. "You really... you don't want to come home?"

"I'll be here," I say. "You can visit me."

Snowy nods, her face solemn. She takes me by the shoulders and kisses my forehead. "Be good." She gives me a sad smile. "I'll miss you. But not your hair."

I laugh. I guess I'll miss her too. But not her tower. Or her rules. Or her stories. Or her scolding. Maybe I won't miss her at all.

"Bye Snowy," I say.

Hunter steps forward and puts his arm around her shoulders. He aims his wand downward and shoots at the ground. In a burst of golden light, they both vanish.

I head back inside the palace. I'm not sad. But I feel weird, like something has ended. Maybe it's just nerves. But I can't shake the feeling that Snowy is gone and I'm not going to see her again.

Chapter 35

We have supper together that evening – me, Beauty,
Lunilla, Cooper, Melodie, and Kay. Thankfully, it's a long
table with wide spaces between our chairs. The king and
queen sit at the narrow ends of the table. I sit opposite
Beauty, Kay sits opposite his mother. But one chair and
setting remains empty.

Beauty points it out first. "Where's she?"

"Who?" I know who but I feel like bugging her.

Beauty exhales. "The... snow lady!"

"Oh. She left." I poke at my food. It's actually really
good, slices of beef in a thick sauce with mushrooms. I
guess Snowy wasn't a great cook because I think everything here tastes amazing.

"What do you mean, she left?" Lunilla barks at me.
She's worn a scowling-toad face all afternoon.

"I mean she's not here anymore," I say dryly. I'm not
going to tell them what happened. Let them wonder.

"Goodness, I never even saw her," Melodie says. She sips her water and sets it down. "I admit, I was curious to meet the Ice Witch."

"The Snow Queen," I say.

"Well, she's neither of those anymore!" Lunilla says. "She's nothing!"

I bristle at this. Snowy isn't nothing. Snowy is Snowy.

Kay stares at his mother. "Hey, you sound a lot better today. You're not coughing."

"I do feel better." Melodie pats her chest. "The cook made me a strong herbal broth last night. I think it's helping."

Oh sugar, I'm dying to tell her! And someday I will. But right now, I don't want most of them knowing I cry magic tears. They might try to make me prove it and I really don't feel like crying just now, especially not in front of Beauty. Melodie looks so much healthier, her eyes have lost that sunken look and her skin is a fresher color. I never get to see the results of my magic and I'm feeling proud.

I spear another slice of beef with my fork, and with my left hand, make the motion of playing chords on the table. My feet shift to imaginary pedals.

"Is there an organ here?" I ask. I just realized how much I miss playing, it's been days. My fingers are itching for it.

Lunilla shrugs. But Cooper says, "Yeah, there's one in the king's old room."

180

I stare at him. "What?"

"In the king's room. King Edgar. I guess he played."

"He did?" Beauty and I say together.

"Looks like it, he had lots of sheets with music stuff on it," Cooper says. "Bunch of gibberish to me."

"Where? Where is it?" I cry. This is amazing!

"Kay can show you after supper," Cooper says.

"I'd like to see it, too," Beauty says and I'm surprised at the eagerness in her voice. "Do you mean this was our father's bedroom?"

"One of them, he had a bunch," Cooper says. "This one's in the main tower. Might've been his favorite, we found a lot of his clothes and books in there. Maybe it was a place to go when the wife was angry." He gives a rough laugh and looks at Lunilla.

"Or just another place to take his *women*," Lunilla says. "He was disgusting, just what Cindy deserved."

Beauty looks offended. "I don't believe you."

"You're just jealous because she got the prince and you didn't!" I say. "I know the ball story, Snowy told it to me."

"The ball story?" Beauty says.

"I didn't want the prince!" Lunilla laughs. "Not even Cindy wanted him once she found out how he was. We had to force her!"

"You what?" I say.

"Lunilla, don't," Melodie says. "They don't need to hear about that, it was a mistake."

"What did you force her to do?" Beauty asks.

Melodie holds up a hand to stop an outburst from Lunilla and answers herself. "In a way, we forced Cindy to marry the prince. She didn't want to, she was afraid of him. We thought it would bring prestige to our family – at least, that's what our mother thought."

"But Cindy ruined everything, like she always did!" Lunilla says. "I hope she rots in that box for eternity."

Beauty's finely-curved eyebrows drop low. She sets down her fork and shifts in her chair to face Lunilla. "As soon as I'm queen, I want you out of this palace. You are never to come back here."

Lunilla snorts. "I'm not going anywhere."

"Oh, but you are," Beauty says. "After tomorrow, this will be *my* kingdom. All of you will have to leave."

"All of us?" Kay asks.

"Well... not *that* one." Beauty flicks her lashes at me. "But only because Godnutter wants her here."

"How kind of you," I say with sarcasm.

Kay squirms in his chair. "But what about-"

"Oh hush, Kay, hush!" Beauty throws up her hands. She closes her eyes and releases a long sigh. "Godnutter came to see me in my room, she had one more thing to say." Beauty sighs again. "She said... she said I have to let you be the king."

Kay sits straighter. "She did?"

"I'm *not* going to marry you!" Beauty says. "So, don't even try that with me. Godnutter and I had a huge fight and this is the compromise. I'll be the queen and you'll be the king, but you and I are not together!"

"That's not how it's done," Cooper says.

"I can live with this!" Kay says, clearly delighted. "It's a little weird but we can make it work."

Ugh, I can almost read his thoughts. He'll take it because it means he can be with Beauty. Give him another chance with her. As if that'll change anything! I want to shake him, I want to smack his stupid head.

"What's the reason behind this?" I ask.

"Well...." Beauty strokes back her hair in that self-caressing way. "She said we can't do a public ceremony, there isn't time to prepare the kingdom. It'll have to be a small, private affair, but I can have a few friends. The kingdom at large will not be told right away. Little by little, we'll let the word spread that there's a new queen. But Godnutter thinks they'll accept this more readily if Kay is the king because the people *know* Kay. And they don't know me. I don't like it but she's got a point."

"I think it's a great idea!" Kay says.

"And what about us?" Lunilla barks out. "Won't the people want to know what HAPPENED to us?"

"And will I get to stay with my son or am I banished too?" Melodie asks.

"Oh crackers, you know what? I don't care!" Beauty says. "I'll let Godnutter deal with you, I have other things to worry about. Like finishing my dress. I need more straw brought to my room so I can keep spinning. I have two spools done, ten more left to do."

"Why on earth are you spinning straw?" Melodie asks.

"On a spinning wheel?" Kay cries.

Beauty rolls her eyes and blinks at least four times. "My birthday won't be until the end of next month! It's perfectly safe!"

I bite my lip to hold back a smile. I don't know why she's got that wrong but she's got that wrong. And I can use it. *I* know when our birthday is.

Lunilla stands up. "I'm not listening to any more of this. I'm going to see Jack." She flounces away from the table but turns to give a sharp eye to Cooper. He rises and follows her.

Once they're gone, Kay leans on the table and looks across at Beauty. "They're going to do something, you know that, right?"

Beauty shrugs. "They can't do anything to me."

I look down at my lap and bite my lip harder. They're not the ones you need to worry about, Beauty.

Chapter 36

I shut myself in my room after supper. I just couldn't stand Kay's obsession with his Beauty queen anymore. He looked so happy with the new arrangement.

The night is strange. My two servant ladies gave me a nightgown, tucked me into bed, and blew out the candles. Then they left me alone in that huge, dark room. The bed is soft and smells like flowers. But Snowy isn't there. I'm used to sleeping with my elbow touching the curve of her back, or her chilly foot against my lower leg. I don't like all this space in my bed. This whole palace has way too much space.

I wish Hunter hadn't taken her away. Snowy was... my person. I mean – Kay has his mother to go to. Lunilla has Cooper. Beauty has Godnutter, I guess. But I just lost my person. No one in this palace will be looking out for me. I'm on my own, now.

If I don't get rid of Beauty, this is how it'll always be. She'll be the queen and I'll be... like Melodie. The sister no one cares about, the one who gets forgotten. The one that Kay comes to see when Beauty pushes him away. Second best.

I did not escape my tower to be second best.

One more day. I've got to deal with this for one more day. Then, if everything goes right, they'll be putting the crown on my head instead of hers.

▪▪

After breakfast, Kay takes me and Beauty to see the room that belonged to my father. Like Cooper said, it's a tower room, much larger than what I'm used to, but the roundness feels familiar and comforting. There's a large window just opposite the door, wider than both of my arms stretched out, with a low ledge for sitting on. I wish my tower at home had a window like that, it gives so much cheery light to the room.

It looks like he came here to relax. There are chairs with pillows and footstools, shelves full of books, a desk covered with drawings of bears or wolves – did my father draw? – and several pairs of boots lying around. And the organ. Gasping, I rush over to it. It looks much different than mine, much fancier. The whole thing is encased in ornamental wood and the pipes are a dark golden color. Gently, I press a finger to one of the smooth, white keys. Nothing. No sound comes out. You're kidding me, right?

186

I try a few more keys without success. What a horrible disappointment – it doesn't work anymore.

Behind me, I hear Beauty gasp. "Is that him?"

"Hmm?" Kay says. "Oh yes, that's him. And his first wife, I believe."

I rush over to Beauty. She's staring at a painting that hangs over the desk with my father's drawings. I hadn't noticed it before - I was looking for the organ. There are two people in the painting. One is a woman who is dressed like a queen and sits in a fancy chair. She has smooth, black hair and looks so much like Snowy, it creeps me out. I guess that was her mother. The one who came before Cinderella.

A man stands behind her, one hand resting on the top of the chair. So, this is my father, King Edgar. A tall, slim man with pale yellow hair. Like the queen, he barely smiles. But there's laughter in his proud blue eyes, in the taunting lift of one eyebrow. Oh, I like him. I like him very much.

Beauty seems to share my thoughts. She grins up at the painting, her cheeks flushed. "He's a fine-looking man, don't you think?"

I nod, amazed that we agree on something.

Her smiles sags, just a little. "Do you think... do you think if he was here now, if he could see us.... Do you think he would...."

"What?" I say.

Beauty shakes her head. "Nothing. I just wish...." She stares at the painting and her eyes hold a struggle.

"Me too," I say.

Beauty looks at me and her face closes off. "Well, doesn't matter now, anyway. I should get back to my spinning, I have *got* to fill all those spools by tonight. Kay, come with me, I need more straw." She snaps her fingers and Kay runs after her like a dog.

Before leaving the room, I press my fingers to the organ again. What a shame it doesn't work.

I wander downstairs with a thought of going out to the rose garden. In the front hall, I run into Lunilla and Cooper. *And the baby!*

"We're going out, now that the weather's less foul," Lunilla says. "Thought we'd take Jack for a little carriage ride." She smiles in such a friendly way, I'm taken aback.

"May I - may I look at him?" I ask breathlessly. She smiles and shifts the baby in her arms so I can see him better.

I feel like everything inside me goes quiet. He is so small, it feels like a wondrous miracle. I stare at his tiny face and perfect little hands, curled up. He has a thin fuzz of brownish hair and dark eyes that blink at me as if he can't figure me out. Then he yawns and I burst into laughter for no reason.

"Oh, I love him! I love babies!" I say. I know about babies and children but I never saw one up close, before. Now I want to see more, I want to know what children are like. Small people, it sounds so wonderful.

Lunilla smiles with pride. Then Cooper clears his throat and she says, "We'd better go. I want Jack to enjoy the air before he falls asleep. Tell the others not to worry if we're back late."

I nod and watch them walk out the door. Tell the others, she said. Who are the others? I change my mind about going to the rose garden and decide to look for Melodie. Maybe she can help me figure out why the organ isn't working. I'm still yearning to play. I don't know why I'm going to her – or maybe I do. I guess, in some ways, she reminds me of Snowy.

I find her in the throne room. She's standing near that weird, glassy chair, speaking to a few servants. She directs them to bring in more candlesticks, hang some banners on the walls, and fill a bunch of vases with red roses. I walk over to her, holding my braid off the floor.

"What are you doing?" I ask.

Melodie looks at me. "Decorating. For the coronation, tomorrow." Her voice is still bored, that hasn't changed.

"You are?"

"Beauty asked me to do it. I don't mind. She's too busy with the spinning to do it herself. Wants a lot of red roses, that was her only direction."

"Lunilla went out and said not to worry."

"Went where?"

I shrug. "She said for a carriage ride. Cooper and the baby went with her."

"All of them?" Melodie's tone gets sharper. "Are you sure?"

"I saw them leave. But she said not to worry."

Melodie presses her mouth into a hard line. "That's a bad sign. It's the day before she's being deposed as queen. Does that sound like the time to take a pleasure drive to you?"

"What?"

"Excuse me." Melodie steps past me and walks swiftly out of the throne room.

Oh sugar. I forgot to ask about the organ.

Chapter 37

Feeling kind of bored and kind of lonely, I begin the opening doors game. This means that I walk around the palace, open doors and look inside. It's fun for a while; I see a lot of strange furniture. I think I even find the room where that creepy mirror was. But after a while, it gets boring. The rooms where the servants work are more interesting; I like watching them cook and wash and iron. They smile but otherwise take no notice of me.

I'm starting to get frustrated but I remind myself I have only to get to the end of this day. Like waiting for Snowy to come home with gingerbread, it feels like it's never going to happen. I hate waiting. By late afternoon, I'm starting to go crazy.

I've left the kitchen and I'm wandering along a dim corridor. Near the end, I wrench open a heavy door and find steps going down. A dank smell rises up to me and my stomach clenches - the dungeon. I'm about to slam the door shut but I stop myself. I'm not a prisoner, now. I can look if I want to.

I'm just curious about the place where Snowy got in. She mentioned a secret tunnel – I'd like to see that. I grab the nearest wall torch and hook my thick braid over my elbow. With a shaky heart, I head down the cracked stone steps.

A low corridor, dark as night. Those doors made of metal bars. I don't hear any sounds as I walk between the cells, maybe Beauty and I were the only prisoners. It's much longer than I thought; I count fourteen cells on one side as I go. But it ends with a flat stone wall in my face. I don't see a secret passage at all. I try rapping the wall with my knuckles but that hurts.

I turn back, annoyed. The first door on the opposite wall catches my eye. It's solid wood, unlike the other doors, and separated from them by a greater distance. Maybe Snowy's secret passage is in there.

The door resists. It grunts and groans as I bump my shoulder against it and dust falls all over me when it gives. I brush off my head and peer around.

I'm inside a large room, very dirty, very cobwebby. I don't understand half of what's in here. Shelves, jars, tables cluttered with strange objects, and a giant black pot in the middle of the room. I've never seen a pot that huge, you could cook all of me inside it. Everything I see is coated with rubble and dust.

I walk around, my nose crinkled. The smells are strange, I don't recognize them. Dust and decay but other smells underneath. Must be coming from the jars on the shelves. I can't tell what was in them, it's all dried up and black.

I stop by a wooden stand with a thick book on top. It's the only book I see in this room. I lean in and blow the thick blanket of dust off the cover. My eyes widen as I read the title: *Book of Spells.*

I hold my breath. Really? Is this really a book of spells? I shift the crackling torch to my other hand and open the cover with one finger.

I don't know how long I stand there. My torch shrinks until I fear it will burn my hand but I can't stop reading. It's the most fascinating thing I've ever seen. It describes not only spells but also their origins and the world of magic. It tells you how to draw on magic from within yourself to cast spells. Many people struggle to find their inner magic and some doubt they have it at all. But I know I have it, it's in my tears. I read the strange ingredients, the procedures for various spells, and look around me again. I'm starting to understand what this room was for.

One spell sounds like the answer to all my problems. The Forgetting Spell. Often given in food, whoever consumes it will forget their past life entirely. They will believe only what the spellcaster tells them – who they are, where they came from, what they care about. It calls for the use of blue rose petals, like the ones we have in our garden. I can't help it, I think of Kay. If I could make him forget Beauty.... If I could tell him I'm his only friend, the only one he cares about....

I tear the page out before going upstairs for supper. I want to bring the whole book but I'll have to do that in secret. I don't want anyone else knowing about this.

Beauty eats quickly, fretting that she still has five spools left to spin. "I ache all over, my back, my arms, my legs.... Why does it have to be so hard just to get a little gold? I'll going to be up all night with this spinning."

"Wear something else," Kay says. "You don't need a gold dress."

"Yes. I do." Beauty spits the words at him. "I'm going to be queen! Think that happens every day? This is *my* coronation and I want a gold dress. I have to be the most glamorous queen anyone has ever seen."

"Then let's put it off a day," Kay says. "Ask your godmother for more time, we can wait."

"No, we can't!" Beauty says. "I sent out messages to fifty of my friends. Godnutter was mad but I don't really care. I want *some* people to be at my coronation! It still counts as a small one."

I can't taste my chicken anymore. Did she say fifty? Beauty has fifty friends? I want to hurl my plate at her, leap across the table and grab her throat, shriek and yell and scratch her face. Fifty friends! All I have is Kay and he doesn't even want me!

I'm panting through my nose and my teeth are clenched. Calm down, Zelly, don't let them see. If I've been counting the days right, there's just a few more hours to go. And then everything Beauty has will be mine.

Melodie, who has barely spoken during the meal, turns to her son. "Kay, I think we should leave the palace tonight. And I think Beauty and Rapunzel should come with us."

"Why?" we all cry together.

"Lunilla hasn't come back. And it bothers me."

"She said not to worry," I say.

"That's what bothers me. I don't think she's *coming* back," Melodie says.

"Where would she go?" Kay asks.

"I don't know. She's been insane with rage that her throne is being taken. It was always her greatest fear. I don't think she just went for a drive, I think she's doing something."

"Like what?" I ask.

Melodie's face is tight. "I think she's going to attack in some way. With the coronation tomorrow, tonight would be the night to do it. We should leave."

"She wouldn't hurt us," Kay says. "We're family."

"There is nothing my sister wouldn't do," Melodie says. "She wants the throne for herself. And later for Jack. She will not give that up, not even for you, Kay."

Beauty smirks. "She can't do a thing. Godnutter told her she can't do a thing."

"Did you always do everything your godmother told you?" Melodie asks. "Did you listen, even when you saw a way out?"

Beauty shuts her mouth.

But we *can't* leave!" I cry. Or my plans are ruined. "That means we're letting Lunilla win. This palace has plenty of guards, right? They'll protect us!"

"And Aunt Lunilla can't do magic," Kay says.

"Maybe she's giving up," Beauty says. "Rather than being kicked off her throne, she's running away before we can do it."

Melodie shakes her head. "That's not Lunilla."

"Doesn't matter!" I say fiercely. "I'm not going anywhere. If the rest of you want to run away, fine! They can crown *me* tomorrow." I glare at Beauty, knowing that will seal the deal.

She narrows her eyes at me. "Over my dead body."

Melodie looks at Kay. Very gently, he shakes his head. Melodie throws down her fork and leaves the table.

Chapter 38

I go to my room after supper. When my two servant ladies come to dress me for bed, I dismiss them, saying I don't need their help tonight. I take my favorite warm blue dress out of my wardrobe cabinet and lay it over a chair. This is what I want to be crowned queen in. Once Beauty is gone, they'll have to choose me. And Kay will be my king. With this new spell, I'll make him forget she ever existed. Everything will be perfect.

I sit on the bed and pull out the folded page from the inside of my dress. I read the spell over and over until I'm sure I'm memorized it. Just in case I lose the paper or something. I practice until I can recite it with my eyes shut. *Make thyself a tempting brew, start with a kettle of morning dew. Add maple sugar and honey, too. The petals of roses, brightest blue....*

Blue roses. I should get them now, I don't know how long they're going to bloom. But it's still too early. I hear movements in the hall outside my room, the occasional voice. No one has gone to bed yet. The minutes pass like syrup, one sluggish drop at a time. I'm waiting for midnight. When it's midnight, today becomes tomorrow. And tomorrow is the day I need.

I pull open a drawer in a small table beside my bed to hide the paper. Inside the drawer, I find a pouch with a drawstring to keep it shut. Interesting. Snowy has one just like it, she uses it to carry coins. I take the pouch and shut the drawer. I'll use this to hold the roses.

I find a book and climb back onto the bed. It's hard to focus but I try and force myself to read. I have a few more hours to kill. At least the book is good, after a while I'm really into it. It tells the story of a man who rescues a bunch of children from their cruel village where they had to work hard and were never allowed to play. He plays his pipe and the children follow him to a wonderful new land. There are drawings of the happy, skipping children and I find myself grinning over them. They're so cute and little and they seem to adore the piper. I think that's what I want next, I want to see children.

After I finish the book, I unravel the fancy braid my two servant ladies gave me, brush out all of my hair, and braid it up again, the simple way I've always done it. It always takes two hours to brush and braid my hair, so it's a good time passer. I stand in the middle of the room and arrange my braid in a swirl around my feet, admiring how the candlelight throws bits of gold into the red weave. I love my hair. It may be a pain sometimes but I'm never going to cut it. When I'm queen, I bet the girls of this kingdom will be crazy about my hair. They'll start growing out their own to look like mine.

By now, heavy night has fallen. The windows are black and I don't hear any sounds. Perhaps I can go. I lift the drawstring pouch off the bed and loop the cord around my wrist. Then, carefully, I slip out of my door.

Feeling like some kind of thief, I creep down through the palace. I'm wearing soft lady-shoes that the housekeeper gave me and they're much quieter than Snowy's boots. A tired-looking servant passes me with a bucket but otherwise, I see no one.

I slip out to the rose garden through a door near the kitchen, the one Lunilla showed me. And I stop. It's warm out here! Warm as soup. I don't remember the air ever feeling like this.

Oh sugar, I forgot to bring a light with me. But the moon is nearly full and I can make out the rose bushes, though they look like scruffy black shapes. I remember where the blue ones were, about midway up this row. I creep along the path, holding my braid like a baby in my arms. It makes too much noise when it drags.

I check the roses by sniffing. Yes, these are the blue ones, the smell is calming. I throw a quick glance over my shoulder at the palace. A few windows are glowing like gold teeth in the wall. Not everyone is asleep yet. Quickly and quietly, I pinch four roses off the bush and push them into the small bag hanging from my wrist. As I close the bag, a pool of light falls over me.

"Zelly?"

I spin around. Kay is right behind me with a lantern in his hand.

Chapter 39

"Oh. Hi Kay."

"Hi. Why are you out here in the dark?"

"I forgot a candle."

He smiles as if amused but his eyes do not sit on me easily. He's remembering our fight. "Are you looking for something?"

"Are you?" I lower my arm so he won't notice the bag dangling from my wrist.

Kay shrugs. "Nothing much." He steps around me and heads up the path, carrying his lantern. He stops when he reaches a bush full of blood-red roses. As he stares at them, he sighs.

"What's wrong?" I say.

"Nothing. You'll just get mad."

"Is it about Beauty?"

"Yes."

He's right. I'm getting mad. I cast a scornful glance down on the bush. "Getting her a rose?"

"She wants it," he says. "I asked if I could give her something for the coronation tomorrow. She said a red rose for her hair. But...." He rubs a hand over his tired face. "She said it impatiently, like she just wanted to get rid of me."

"And yet you are still getting the rose," I say dryly. He's cutting it off the bush with his knife, leaving a long section of stem attached. He walks back up the path to me with it.

"I'm trying to be hopeful," he says. "But it's hard. I was excited at first, the two of us crowned together. I thought it would give me more time with her, let her get to know me."

"I figured," I say.

"But now...." Kay turns the rose in his hand. "This is how it's going to be, isn't it? She's going to push me away, even when I'm king. I still won't be good enough for her."

"No, you won't," I say harshly. I'm not sugar-coating Beauty. I walk up the path without lifting my braid and it hisses over the dirt behind me. I decide to go in at the front of the palace, I want to check that big clock on the main tower. The wind swoops into my face and I catch an odd smell, but familiar.

I turn around. "Is Barker here?"

"Barker?" Kay looks bewildered.

"Never mind," I say. The smell is gone, I caught only a whiff of it. Earthy and musky, like the cottage. It was odd, that smell, which is why I remember it. And how I heard something moving around above me but came out and found Barker on the stairs.

I leave the garden and walk toward the front of the palace, approaching those white circular stairs from the left. The large clock hangs far above the main doors, a black face with gold hands. Five minutes to midnight. It's nearly time.

Kay catches up to me. "Zelly... look. I know I haven't been a good friend. But I still like you! And I thought you liked me, too."

"I did. But...." We stop at the base of the stairs and I put a hand on my hip. "Here's the thing, Kay. I *do* like you. I like the way you talk to me. I like your teeth when you smile and I like your eyebrows. I like it that you make me laugh, because I never laugh at all. You don't have to convince me to like you, I just do! You are... my first friend, Kay. I've been waiting all my life for you."

I was going to say more but gob dash it, my throat tightens up. I was going to say that if Beauty doesn't feel like that, she doesn't deserve him. But I think he got it. Because he reaches out and pulls me against him.

I wasn't expecting it. The warmth, the closeness, the strangeness of it. My cheek is against his chest and it feels squarish and firm. His arms press on my back, his hands squeeze my shoulders, and all I can think is that being trapped in a small space has never felt so wonderful. I breathe deeply, inhaling his scent. And he smells so good, like... like Kay.

His face is bowed over me and I feel his chin settle on top of my head. "What a jerk I've been."

"No, you haven't." My voice comes out soft as a dove. "You've just been distracted."

"I never told you..." Kay steps back and shines his white smile all over me "...how beautiful your hair is. I've always admired it."

"Really? You like my hair?" I grin and brush it lightly with my fingers. My chest fills up with a happy, glowing feeling.

"It's amazing, the color of fire when it's burning low in the hearth. I always thought fire was beautiful and your hair reminds me of it. Don't ever cut it, please, I'd be heartbroken!"

I laugh. He likes my hair! I plop myself down on the marble steps and pat the place beside me. "Sit down, Kay. We haven't really talked in a while." I forgot how much I like talking to Kay when it's not about Beauty.

Kay smiles and sits next to me, resting his arms on his knees. He looks relaxed now, even happy. Happy to be with me. "All right," he says. "You want to go first?"

BONG....

Oh my blood and bones. The clock.

BONG....

It's midnight. It's time. But now, I don't want to leave Kay.

BONG....

I jump to my feet. "Stay here! I'll be right back!"

"Where are you going?"

"I have to do something real quick."

BONG....

Kay smiles. "Sure, Zelly. Don't be long!"

I fly up the white marble steps. *BONG....* It's time. It's time. I'm nervous but I feel like cheering. Kay and I are friends again. *BONG....* With the possibility – perhaps – of being something more? The way he grinned at me just now sent my heart to the skies. I want to feel that again.

BONG....

I dash into the palace. Up corridors and stairs without being aware of them. *BONG.... BONG....* The clock is like a massive heart, beating out the sound of my fear. Because I am afraid, now. I know what I'm going to do is wicked.

BONG....

Just get it over with. Quickly as possible. Then Kay will be mine. He'll forget about Beauty, I'll see to that. It's going to be fine.

I skid into Beauty's chamber. It's dark - she's still on the balcony, spinning in the weak light of one candle. Her back faces me through the open glass doors.

BONG....

I don't hesitate. I rush out on the balcony and grab her wrist, yanking her hand off the machine. She gasps and looks at me. I see the spindle, holding its spool of golden thread. The point is so beautifully sharp.

Still clutching her wrist, I lean in and stare into her perfect blue eyes. "Happy Birthday, Beauty!" I hiss out. And then I thrust her hand down on the sharp spindle point.

BONG....

Chapter 40

Beauty shrieks and jumps off the chair, jerking out of my grasp. "Are you CRAZY?" She opens her hand and there's a thick drop of blood growing out of her middle finger. She stares at it and then raises murderous eyes to my face. Her mouth opens... but I'll never know what she might have said.

Because Beauty drops, right there on the balcony. Close to the spinning wheel, almost curled against it. Her long lashes flutter for a moment. Then she lies still.

I step back, covering my mouth. Oh my blood and bones, I did it! She's gone now, gone! Not dead but gone from my life. And no one will know it was me. I'll pretend to be as shocked as everyone else. I'll go down to Kay now and act like nothing happened. And we'll have our talk. Slowly, I creep around Beauty's fallen figure, trying to wipe off the cold sweat that's sprung out on me.

Something trembles. I feel it first in my feet. Then a low, grumbling sound reaches my ears. I freeze on the balcony and spread my arms for balance as the trembling increases. Could it be the whole palace is shaking?

I spin around and look out. It's too dark to see. But the land has awakened with terrible sounds of cracking and crunching, like the earth is splitting, like trees are falling, like stone is crushing against stone. The tremor worsens and I tumble onto the balcony railing. Slumped over it, I stare at the ground below. The moonlight gives me a feeble impression of something long and many-armed that seems to be climbing out of the earth. My eyes jump to the palace wall where a tendril of – ivy, is it ivy? – shoots up past me, slithering like a snake. And that does it.

Screaming, I run inside the palace, jerking my braid into my arms. The shaking throws me off balance and I topple onto one knee. Wrenching myself up, I race out of Beauty's room and down the hall to my own. I hurl myself onto the bed, sweep the blankets over me, and cry and cry and cry. This is the worse, most horrible day of my life. Happy Birthday, Rapunzel.

In my terror, I don't know how much time passes. Possibly, a few minutes but it feels like hours. The shaking stops, the rumbling stops. Everything becomes quiet again. But I don't come out from under my blanket.

Then I hear a low, cutting voice right in front of me. *"What did you do?"*

I throw the blanket off my head. Godnutter stands in front of me, just behind the footboard. She glows like a giant flame in the dark bedroom. I lift an arm to shield myself, nearly blinded from her brilliance. Her eyes are wide open, bulging with rage.

I cower back on the bed. "I didn't know!"

"NO!" She points her pipe at me. "You knew *exactly* what you were doing! You knew her real birthday!"

"Why didn't she?" I cry.

"Because *I* didn't know it!" Godnutter shouts. "I was away when Cinderella gave birth, the stupid fairies had called me in! I wasn't sure of the exact day. I celebrated Beauty's birthday on the day I brought her home. Why do you think I was in such a rush to have her crowned? I knew her real birthday was sooner than she thought, I knew there was danger. I just didn't expect it to come from you!"

"I hated her!" I cry. "She ruined everything!"

"If you weren't Cinderella's other child, I would kill you right now for this. She was your sister! My child! I raised her myself!"

"And you did a lousy job! She was a nasty brat!"

"You're no treat yourself, tootsie," Godnutter snaps. "Mark my words, you will suffer for this! In every way I can think of. I won't take your life but I'll start with..." her eyes fall to my braid lying in loops around me on the bed "...your hair."

I grab at my braid with both hands. "No!"

"Oh, I'm sorry. Is it special to you? Well, that's what Beauty was to me. My little Beauty, that's what I always called her. That's how she got her name. I was proud of her, she reminded me of her mother. And now you've curse her! Goodness only knows how long she's going to lie there-"

As she says these last words, she turns and gestures in the direction of Beauty's room. Her turned back gives me a moment of opportunity and I take it. My hands still cling to my hair, with a loose section of five or six feet bridged between them. When Godnutter turns her head, I fling the braid up and out, looping it around her neck. She spins back to me but I yank the braid down, hard as I can, throwing all of my weight into it. Godnutter's head jerks downward and her forehead strikes the footboard with a solid CRACK! She topples out of sight behind the bed.

Chapter 41

I wait, breathless, every muscle tensed and ready. I hear nothing. I slide off the bed, towing my hair with me, and rush forward. I feel like I'm going to pass out from fear.

Godnutter is on the floor. She lies on her back, one knee up, wings spread beneath her. Her eyes are shut and a dark lump is forming on her forehead. One arm rests on her chest, the other at her side, and by this arm I see, in the folds of her dress, the pipe lying free.

With shaky breaths, I crouch and pick up the pipe. Is she dead? I can't tell and don't want to find out. I leave the room as fast as I can. I have to get away from here in case she wakes up.

I'm in the hall when I see the first two bodies. Lying within a few feet of my door, barely noticeable in the dark - my two servant ladies. On the floor, one slumped over the other. Were they coming to check on me? Why are they both passed out?

I hurry down a set of stairs to the floor below. And I find another one. A servant man, who I've noticed goes around the palace at night, dousing all the candles. He's lying on the floor with the snuffer still in his fingers.

I don't understand. Ready to panic, I rush upstairs and search out Melodie's room. I enter without knocking, hoping to find her in bed. But she's not, she's over by the window... on the floor.

I throw myself down beside her. "Melodie! Melodie!" I shake her shoulder, desperate for any response. But I get nothing. I pull back, feeling like I'm going to throw up. Is she dead? Are they all dead? Did the earthquake kill them? Suddenly, she draws a sigh in her sleep and I gasp with relief. All right. Not dead, at least.

My eyes rise to the window and I gasp again. There are vines, thick, twisted vines pressed against the glass. Only small bits of moonlight glow between them. I rise, knowing this is something new, and step closer. It's a tangle of dense, ugly vines with hooked thorns. Growing way up here, many floors above the ground.

I wander around the palace to confirm my fears. As I guessed, everyone is unconscious and those horrible vines cover every window. That must have been what caused the crunching and shaking, the vines breaking through the earth and rising to cover the palace. It happened the moment Beauty pricked her finger, so it must be part of the curse. But why vines? What do they do?

And what about me? Why am I the only one awake? Everyone is under the same curse, I've figured that out by now. But somehow, I was spared. Oh wait! Ohhh.... I remember Hunter tapping me with his magic wand. Giving me a protection spell that would last a few days. Oh my blood and bones. I guess it worked.

Kay! What happened to Kay? I fly down to the first floor, hoping with all my strength that he's still awake. I left him on the stairs, outside the palace. Maybe only the people *inside* were affected.

One of the main doors to the palace stands ajar, as I left it when I rushed in here to curse Beauty. Within seconds, I can see it's useless to get out. The vines have crawled in the gap and twisted around the door, choking all the space. I push on one of the vines but it's thicker than my leg and doesn't budge. "KAY!" I yell through the dense, green jungle. No answer. Am I actually trapped inside the palace? With all of these unconscious people?

I press a hand to my mouth because I think I'm going to scream, and if I do, I know I won't stop. My breaths rush in and out of my nose. I need to calm down. I need something to calm me. I need to find something that will calm me down.

Instinctively, I go for the only object of comfort I can think of: the organ in my father's room. As I creep in, I observe the wide window on the opposite wall. Like all the rest, it's grown over with vines. But my eyes have long since adjusted to the darkness and enough moonlight sneaks in to help me find my way around. I stare at the organ for several minutes, wondering why it doesn't work. Then I notice it has two broad pedals at the base, instead of the log rods I'm used to.

Oh, wait - I get it! This organ isn't like the one in my tower, which has its wind supplied through valves in the wall. Those two pedals are the bellows, I'll have to pump the air into it as I play. I haven't tried this before but I've read about it. Shouldn't be too hard.

I sit on the stool and lay Godnutter's pipe in my lap. My hands find their positions as naturally as birds returning to their nests. I pump the pedals a few times to start the air flowing and then I press the keys with my fingers. The organ groans into life, the sound swelling through the room.

I play a harsh, angry piece I learned earlier this year. It's complicated and I have to concentrate as the notes tumble up and down. My heart begins to settle and my thoughts stop crashing around. I know it's crazy to be playing the organ right now but I've missed it so much. It's the only thing keeping me from total panic.

I play maybe fifteen minutes without stopping. And then pause to rest my arms. My head feels quieter. All right, calmly now. I need to think of a way to get out of here. Maybe I can find a large knife in the kitchen and cut through the vines.

I hear the floor creak behind me and the soft whine of hinges. I spin around on the stool. The door to this room is opening, though I can't see what's behind it. I stiffen and seize the pipe, thinking it's Godnutter. My nose fills with a thick, musky smell and I hear a low growl that freezes my blood. In the darkness, a massive, black shape moves into the room. Taller than me, sort of hunched, and covered in fur.

The Beast has found me.

I jump up from the stool, gasping. The black form shifts and I catch the shimmer of two dark eyes upon me. With a high shriek, I dart to the other side of the room, where the window is. I hear a rough snort and the thump of heavy paws. I feel weight land behind me, a swipe across my back, and suddenly I'm burning with horrible pain. Screaming, I leap onto the window ledge, not knowing where else to go, oddly aware that I feel many pounds lighter. I throw myself against the glass and scream again. Claws like knives sink into my back, a growl thunders inside my head, and I'm crushed on the glass beneath the warm, hairy mass if its body.

And then the glass bursts.

I feel cool air first. The sensation of falling. And then I hit the vines, losing the air from my lungs, getting smacked and struck as I topple my way down. Flares of pain light up in my arms and legs as the thorns slice me open and then – MY EYES! MY EYES ARE ON FIRE! I scream like I've never screamed before. And that's all I remember.

Chapter 42

I don't wake up until daylight. And I'm only aware of it by the glow on my eyelids. When I try to open them, they burn like fire and I scream. My eyes! What happened to my eyes? Did I lose them? With shaking hands, I gently touch the upper lids. No, I feel the bulge of each eyeball, I still have them. They must be badly scratched.

I can't open them. After a few minutes, I roll onto my knees. Whimpering, I reach behind to check my lower back. It's sticky, indicating blood, and too raw to touch. Open wounds, I think. Four slashes across my back.

And then something brushes my elbow - the rough ends of my hair. I sweep it to the front of my shoulder, grip it and slide my hand down. Just above my waist, my hand falls into empty air.

It's gone. My beautiful hair that took a lifetime to grow has been cut off. It must've happened when the Beast sliced at my back. Where is the Beast? I don't think it fell with me. Why didn't it come down here and finish me off? I'm starting to wish it had.

With my eyes still shut, I begin to crawl. And immediately bump my head on those horrible vines. What on earth are they for? I reach out with one hand and feel around until I find a space. I manage to squeeze through but my back is searing with pain and I gain new scratches from the thorns.

I seem to be in a forest of vines, with little room to wriggle between them. But slowly, slowly, I grope my way through. At one point, my hand comes down on an object and with a gasp, I realize I've found Godnutter's pipe. I didn't know it fell with me. I stuff it inside my dress and keep crawling.

It feels like hours before I put out my hand and don't find any vines. I must be past them. I try to stand but my splitting back won't let me. I try to open my eyes, but it's like hot blades jabbing into them. The worst part is that for the brief second they're open, I can't see anything. Nothing but white.

So I crawl, without any idea where I'm going. It's more horrible than you can imagine. My nose tells me I'm in the rose garden. I crawl until I can't smell the blossoms anymore. That must mean I'm out of it. I feel soft dirt beneath my hands and weeds still mushy from melted snow. And then gravel. It pokes into my knees but I can't stand up. I grit my teeth and just try to get across it. And then my hand bumps into something solid and warm.

I gasp. My hand seizes the thing and gropes around to understand. It's a leg! As I search for more, I find an arm and a chest, propped up against the edges of stairs. I gasp again. Is this Kay? My hands slide over his face. A squarish jaw. Short hair, a bit course. Is it him? I lean into his chest and sniff deeply. Yes, it's Kay. Under the curse, like everyone else.

I crouch over him and take into my hands his face that I cannot see. For several minutes, I sob over him and my tears fall freely. I'm so sorry, Kay! I didn't know this would happen! I just wanted you to be my friend. And now I've lost you. The wetness of my tears soothes my eyes a little but does nothing to cure my injury. They don't work on me, they've never worked on me.

I can't bear it. I crawl away from him. The sharp gravel pierces my knees and I force myself, gasping, into a partial stand. Bent like an old woman, I hobble away from the palace, one hand stretched out to feel my way.

Chapter 43

I think night has fallen. It's hard to tell. I've been walking – well, hobbling – for a long time. I know I'm in The Wood, I've bumped into enough trees. I carry on, with a vague idea of going back to Snowy. But I don't know which way. About two hours ago, I tripped over another unconscious person. So, the curse has struck even those outside the palace. Does that mean Snowy too? It probably does.

Here and there, I try to use the pipe. When I flick it with my wrist, it gives a shudder and something bursts from the other end. Moments later, I smell a tree burning. That seems to be all I can do but it's a start. And I still have the blue roses in the bag on my wrist. I didn't lose them in the fall. Maybe if I eat them, I'll forget what happened to me.

I can't... see. I'm *blind*. All my life, I have hated blindness, feared it more than anything. All my life, I just wanted to escape my tower and *see* the world.

There are so many things I have never seen. And now I never will.

I have tried, several times, to open my eyes. It makes me squeal every time. Little by little, I'm able to assess my vision. It's like trying to look through a window that's been frosted over with snow. A few patches of color get through but it's all very pale and shapeless. The loss of my sight – and my hair – is too much for me. I understand, now, why Snowy threw herself from that tower.

My nose picks up a familiar smell. Ah... I'm close to the cottage where Barker lives. Wood smoke and stewed beef. I trace the smell until my feet find the flagstones leading up to the door. It opens when I push it. And immediately, the musky smell of the Beast fills my head.

My stomach constricts but I understand now. This is where they were keeping it. I heard its footsteps above me the day I was here. Barker must have been told to guard it. Where is he? Probably passed out somewhere, either inside or out back, where my poor mother lies in her box. I'll never see her again, either.

Lunilla let the Beast out, I'm sure of it. I think that's what she did yesterday. Came here, released the Beast, then fled to a far-off place with her husband and child, trusting the Beast to kill us all. Did she think it would kill Godnutter as well? That seems a stretch. Although, I've discovered a fairy can be hurt.

The Beast was there last night when I spoke to Kay in the garden. I smelled it but didn't realize. It must've gotten into the palace when everyone – guards and all – fell under the curse. Just before the vines began to grow. And then I stupidly played the organ and led it right to me. That fact that it hasn't chased me out here means – I think – that it's still inside the palace. Could it not get past the vines? Or are there enough sleeping bodies lying around that it didn't need me as its next meal?

I doubt it's coming back, now that it has a whole palace to run around in. But I shudder to think of those people – and my two servant ladies – lying unprotected. Even so, I have to stay here. I'm lucky I found this place at all, I could've wandered until I starved to death. I'm starving already but there must be food here. Probably nothing fancy. I would kill for a loaf of gingerbread.

I hobble into the cottage, groping my way along the walls. My foot bumps something hard and I feel out the shape of a rocking chair. I lower myself in, moaning and whimpering at the pain in my back. A tear drops along the side of my nose.

I catch the tear with my finger. Then I lift the pipe with my other hand. Carefully, I scrape my forefinger across the edge of the bowl, until I feel fairly certain the tear has fallen inside it. I thought about this a short while ago, adding my magic to Godnutter's. Maybe then, the pipe will work better for me.

A brush of air hits my face – I left the front door open. I can feel the direction it came from. I point the pipe that way, wish for the door to close, and give a flick of my wrist. I feel a burst of energy from the tip of the pipe. Two seconds later, I hear the door snap shut.

I smile though I don't feel a drop of happiness. All the kingdom sleeps, except me. But the curse won't last forever, Hunter said so. I'll use this time to learn magic, to make myself powerful. So powerful, they will fear me even more than they feared Snowy. I don't have to be the queen or live at the palace. This cottage is so much smaller and simpler, better for me in my new condition. I'll find a way to protect the cottage, make it so fearful, no one will ever come near it.

I may be blind but I found my magic. No longer am I the innocent child, trapped inside my tower. No longer am I the lonely girl, desperate to find a friend. No longer am I the pathetic princess, unwanted as the next queen. Oh no. Those silly girls are dead. I know who I am now.

I am the Witch of The Wood.

Coming Next:

Bad Beauty

Join the Mailing List to receive updates and alerts when the next book is released.

http://www.anitavalleart.com/mailinglist.html

About the Author

I always thought the original story of Rapunzel started well and ended strangely. I loved the idea of the tower and the long hair and the prince climbing up to visit her. But then the witch cuts off Rapunzel's hair and banishes her to the desert, and the heartbroken prince throws himself from the tower and gets blinded by thorns. He wanders around, sad and alone, for a few years until Rapunzel finds him and cures him by crying magic tears into his eyes. Um, what? You never said she had magic tears! Not once in the whole story!

I liked the idea of making Rapunzel's tears more of a thing. It showed she had magic within her, which was handy for this series in which they all need a little bit of it. I also really enjoyed bringing back Lunilla as the new queen! She's such a loud character. The challenge of this book was to blend together the stories of Rapunzel, Snow White, and poor Cinderella still asleep in her box. I'm kind of like Godnutter (minus the pipe). I love my poor, broken Cindy.

If you enjoyed *Rotten Rapunzel*, could you please go to Amazon and write a review for me? Amazon gives greater visibility to books that have a lot of reviews, so every one counts, no matter how short. If you're not sure what to write, I would love to hear what your favorite scene was! I had the most fun writing the scene when Godnutter crashes the party.

Thanks so much for supporting an indie author. God bless you.

-Anita Valle

Books by Anita Valle

Maelyn: The Nine Princesses –1
Coralina: The Nine Princesses –2
Heidel: The Nine Princesses –3
Briette: The Nine Princesses -4
Sinful Cinderella
The Bully Monster
50 Princesses Coloring Book
The Best Princess Coloring Book
Dog Cartoons Coloring Book

For more information, please visit my website:
http://www.anitavalleart.com
or e-mail me: **anitavalleart@yahoo.com**